Pale Green Dot

Justin Groot

Copyright © 2017 Justin Groot
Cover by Madison Porter (@Positron_Dream) and Tiffany Le
All rights reserved.
ISBN-13: 978-1978356979

For everybody who's ever told me "Slow down,"
"Trust your feet," "Use your braaaiiiiin..."

In my defense, it's harder than it sounds.

SPECIAL THANKS TO

Doug Bramlett
James "Dicer214"
Christian Best

1

"There has to be something you can give me."

"No."

"Some tidbit. Some morsel."

"Which part of 'no' is giving you trouble?"

"Jack, I've got a green humanoid allegedly ambling out of the Hawaiian jungle. Hundreds of eyewitnesses. Seasoned soldiers, here, alleging this. I've got paragons of reconnoitering reliability informing me that this person was seven feet tall and a screaming electric green. The color of nuclear waste in cartoons, Jack. One gentleman insisted under polygraph that there were vines sprouting from the green person's footprints."

"Ridiculous."

"If green men really are strolling out of the forest, isn't that something the head of the Coast Guard ought to know about?"

"I have nothing to share at this time."

"Do I look like a reporter?"

"Don."

"Then why are you bullshitting me? I'm just trying to do my job."

"Then do your job."

"Jack."

"And stop fucking with mine."

"Here I was thinking the CIA director's role was to acquire and share intelligence."

"Can we get the check? Miss?"

"Surely, Jack, this is within your job description, what I'm requisitioning here."

"Hello? Miss? Okay, thanks. Thanks, yes, you'll be right over. Right."

"Surely you can point me in a promising direction, at the barest minimum."

"Service at these places is not what it used to be."

"Surely."

"Pleasure as always, Don."

*****

They were insects wriggling beneath a magnifying glass. Insects in tailored suits and silk ties. It was all Toni Davis could do not to smile.

"I don't know, ma'am," said Jack Dano, Director of Intelligence of the CIA.

"What do you know?"

"Something turned him green," said Dano. "Whatever it is, he can talk to it. Telepathically. And he no longer sleeps."

Toni leaned back in her excellent chair. Buffed leather, soft where it was supposed to be soft and firm where it was supposed to be firm. The man beside Dano had clearly been wearing his suit for several days straight. His eyes were bloodshot and wild.

"What did you say your name was?" she asked.

"Dale Cooper, Madam Secretary," said the disheveled man. "I oversee the ranger program."

"You're the one who sent him out there."

"Yes, ma'am."

"Well," said Toni, tossing the report onto her teetering to-do pile, "I suppose you've got him in a cell somewhere?"

The men adopted a stony expression she'd seen a million times before.

"You better not be torturing him," she said.

"Of course not," said Dano.

She squinted. "What, then?"

Dano's mustache gave a nervous spasm.

"Madam Secretary," said Cooper, "we have, presently, less-than-full knowledge of his precise geographic whereabouts, is the thing."

"We lost him," said Dano, and exhaled hard through his nose.

Toni tapped her pen a few times. She retrieved the report from the pile and flipped it open.

"In that case," she said, eyes running down the page, "I suggest you get out there and find him."

*****

Just when he thought the sore spot on his lip was going to heal over, Cooper always managed to bite it again. His bottom teeth angled outward because he'd never worn his retainer as a teenager. For decades he'd just lived with it. He could hardly go back to the orthodontist now.

But the lip thing kept happening. It was worse when he was stressed, because then he forgot to chew carefully, and it only took a few overzealous bites to draw his lip into the line of fire. Then the injured tissue swelled up, making it even harder to avoid biting it again.

When Cooper bit his lip at lunch with Jack Dano, immediately after the trainwreck meeting with the Secretary of State, it was the fourth time in a week. His eyes watered. He stuck a grimy finger in his mouth to gauge the damage. It astounded him that he wasn't bleeding.

"You look awful," said Dano, pausing with a fat wad of spaghetti wrapped around his fork.

"Mrrfghul," said Cooper, probing the tender spot with his tongue.

"When was the last time you slept?"

Cooper pushed his plate away. "On the plane."

Dano tried to figure out how to fit the ball of pasta into his mouth. The problem was the bits of spaghetti dangling off, which positioned themselves inconveniently no matter how he turned his fork.

"Get some rest," said Dano.

Cooper rubbed a stain on his tie. "It's my fault."

"Irregardless."

"I should have told them about the subdermals. Full disclosure, to build trust. Whatever happened to him out there, he found out anyway. The girl's was on the floor in a puddle of blood. Did I tell you that? She cut it out herself."

"Thought you installed them next to the carotid?"

Cooper took a sip of coffee and swallowed hastily as it seared his lip. "Apparently she deemed it worth the risk."

"Not stationing an agent outside the room was pushing your luck," said Dano, wiping sauce from his trim white beard.

"I didn't want them to feel like prisoners."

"Mission accomplished."

"I figured we could always track the subdermals if they ran."

"We'll find them. This is America. They've got nowhere to go."

*****

Vincent Chen watched the Arizona horizon skate past. Everything was a featureless light-blasted brown. The sky shone white-blue. There were no clouds.

"What agency did you say you were with?" asked the

Navajo County sheriff. His fingers around the wheel were gnarled brown roots.

"Not important," said Vincent.

"It's got to do with aliens, don't it."

Vincent shifted, trying to find a position that alleviated his aching shoulder. "No."

"Man reports an alien stole his truck, and you roll up the next day?"

"We've got a warrant on a serial killer who's known to paint himself green."

The sheriff scratched his nose. "How about that."

A sixteen-wheeler whipped by in the opposite lane, a hammer-blow of air and sound. The car shuddered.

"No aliens," said Vincent firmly.

After a while the sheriff slowed the car and turned onto a dirt road. Vincent gripped the edge of his seat. Every rattle jarred his shoulder. Three years and it still hadn't healed, physical therapy be damned.

When they rolled to a stop in front of a ranch house, Vincent shoved the door and stepped out. He quelled an urge to stretch as the owner came out to greet them.

"Howdy, Sheriff," said the rancher, hands resting on suspenders that struggled to contain his enormous belly.

"Vincent Chen," said Vincent.

"Scott Brown," said the man. He shook Vincent's hand, turned, and spat. "About time one of you types made it out here."

"Tell me what happened," said Vincent. He didn't know why the man was faking a Southern accent, and he didn't care.

"Around one o'clock something kicked over the rain bucket. Made a hell of a clatter. Figgered it was an animal."

Vincent spotted something red and moved to investigate. A blood-soaked rabbit lay with legs splayed, a chunk torn out of its middle.

"Yes sir," said the rancher, lumbering over, "that there's where he was. When I turned on the floodlights, he was chowing down. Blood everywhere. Big tiger-type fangs." He demonstrated with his fingers. "Skin green as a grasshopper."

Vincent pulled a pair of latex gloves from his bag.

"Sheriff, you know I ain't the type to leave my shotgun far from hand. And the day I let some alien trespass on my property is the day I vote for Sharia law. Plus I wanted to catch him, you know, just to have some proof."

Scott pointed to a spray of droplets that darkened the ground beyond.

"You hit him," said the sheriff.

"Clipped him in the shoulder," said Scott. "But the bugger made it to my truck."

The sun careened off the sand. Vincent lifted the rabbit's body into a plastic bag.

"Ain't the first time I seen one of them, neither. They're all over these parts. Was blue lights in the sky last summer. And I found a bone out in the boonies what don't belong to nothing terrestrial. I can bring it out, if'n you like. Imagine it'd interest a man of your profession."

"Did he have a companion?" asked Vincent.

"Yes sir. Drove the truck. Definitely another alien." Scott spat again, eagerly. "Want to see that bone?"

"He don't want to see your god damn bone," said the sheriff.

"All due respect, sheriff, I feel it might have some-"

Vincent forked blood-spattered dirt into a second evidence bag and straightened, knees creaking.

"That'll be all," he said.

Scott followed him to the car. "You got one of them mind-erase guns? Pull the trigger and I lose my memory?"

Vincent turned.

"That's what my real gun is for," he said.

As the sheriff drove back down the bumpy road, Vincent lifted the evidence bag and examined the rabbit. He imagined biting into a living animal, the fur and skin giving way, little bones crunching and splintering as hot blood thump-thumped out.

He put the rabbit away and went back to watching the horizon.

*****

Sixteen Hours Earlier

Tetris spotted a sliver of furry movement as he rounded the corner and dove in pursuit. He put a foot down in a bucket and tumbled, but the noise was nothing compared to the locomotive in his head. Kicking free, he muscled up and out of tickling grass as the rabbit cut hard

14

right. Long feet splashed sand into the moonlight. It was dark, but he felt the heat and zeroed in, fingers closing around the thrumming neck. *Snap.* Before his brain caught up, his teeth had plunged into the wonderful hot flesh.

He took three bites before he realized what he'd done.

"Oh God," he mumbled, mouth packed with twitching rabbit.

He swallowed anyway.

Harsh lights snapped on. A window squeaked upward, un-muffling a dog's furious barks, and then the blue-black sky cracked open and something kicked hard against his shoulder, spinning him into the sand. The rabbit slipped through his fingers.

Li shouted from the truck. He staggered up, brain rebooting, concrete feet picking up speed. Blood simmered on his tongue. Another shot sliced the night in half, but this one was well off the mark. He hauled himself into the passenger seat just as Li gunned the engine and pulled away. The door fought back when he tried to close it.

"Your mouth," said Li, punching the light in the ceiling.

He wiped rabbit blood with the back of his good hand. They hit a bump at forty miles an hour and his head smacked the roof.

"I'll pull off the road when we get some space," said Li.

He'd already torn his shirt down the middle, revealing green-tinted torso. Getting the arm out of its sleeve wasn't going to happen. He focused on dragging the seatbelt across his body.

Stop moving.

He ignored the voice and scrabbled the buckle against its silver sheath.

You've got an artery open. I can't close it if you're flailing around.

"Pull over," said Tetris.

"We're not even at the highway," said Li.

"I said pull over."

She hit the brakes. "I don't like that tone."

He pressed himself against the seat as a wad of tentacles wriggled and flexed inside his shoulder. Hands tugged at his sleeve. Li slipped a knife beneath the fabric and neatly opened it. The skin beneath was riddled with holes.

"Buckshot," she said.

We can push that out later. Just bandage it for now.

"Got to stop the bleeding," said Li. "Must have hit your brachial artery."

She flopped half into the back seat and rifled through her pack.

"You're going to owe me five new shirts," she said, grinning, as she pressed cool cloth against his wound.

"Are you enjoying this?"

"Hold," she said, pushing his good hand against the fabric. "I need to see what's wrong with your mouth."

She had her hands on his jaw before he could protest.

"My mouth is fine," he said, jerking away.

The grin vanished. "Your mouth is bleeding."

"It's not my blood."

Oh boy.

"It's not his blood, he says."

"I was eating a rabbit. On accident."

"Why'd you keep telling me you weren't hungry?"

"I *wasn't* hungry."

You're photosynthesizing, said the forest. *But your body needs more than glucose.*

"You've got to be kidding me," said Tetris.

"What?"

"Some kind of craving," he said. "Photosynthesis. Missing nutrients."

Li brushed his hand away and leaned on the wrappings. Blood was streaked across her face like war paint.

"So on top of everything else," she said, "it turned you into a vampire."

Tetris closed his eyes. The forest roamed the confines of his mind like a barely-suppressed memory.

Soon they were back on the highway, blasting toward a gradually-brightening blade of Arizona sky.

2

A cop pulled them over just past the Illinois border. It was four a.m., and Tetris had been driving in silence for hours. Li slept in the passenger seat. Now she sank down, stretching, a predator taking inventory of every sinewy limb. The lights painted her face elaborate patterns of red and blue.

"Fan-fucking-tastic," she said, and slithered out the door, closing it just before the officer came around the corner.

Tetris rolled down his window. "Evening, sir."

The officer directed a flashlight into the cab. Tetris averted his eyes.

"Your taillight's out," said the officer. His hand rested on the smooth grip of a pistol.

"Sorry about that," said Tetris.

"I'll need to see your license and registration."

"They're at home."

Beneath the flashlight beam, Tetris watched the hand on the gun.

"Your face is green," observed the policeman.

"I have a condition."

"You do, huh?"

"Mexican florobotulism. It's quite contagious."

"I'm going to need you to step out of the vehicle."

Tetris stayed where he was. His shoulder throbbed.

"Officer," he said, "I promise to get my taillight fixed at the very earliest opportunity."

"Get out of the vehicle." Fingers slipped around the pistol grip. "Now."

Tetris unbuckled his seat belt. "This is a very bad idea."

The pistol came out of its holster.

"I can't let you arrest me," said Tetris. His heart stomped around in his chest.

"Exit the vehicle and place your hands on your head," said the officer, stepping back as the pistol came up.

Tetris unlatched the door.

Li melted out of the darkness, grabbed a fistful of hair, and smashed the man's face into the upper edge of the open window. Tetris threw himself sideways as the gun discharged. The bullet ripped past his ear. As the cop's cranium rebounded, blood and spittle pinged Tetris's face.

The officer made an animal noise when Li twisted his pistol wrist. The gun dropped. He was significantly larger than her, and when he spun around he knocked her back a few feet, but then Tetris rammed the door hard against his spine.

Li finished him off with a strike to the gut. She had him handcuffed before Tetris was even out of the truck.

*****

Tetris watched the sun rise over flat soybean countryside and a diminishing ribbon of gold-lined highway. With another set of eyes, he watched a tarantula the size of a mobile home make its way through the forest. Pollen shimmered in the air. The spider, moving in nervous bursts, crossed a patch of undisturbed soil.

Pincers erupted from the center of the clearing, followed by a hypertrophied column of iridescent yellow muscle. A worm, hundreds of segments long, each segment edged with tunneling spikes.

The worm snapped its jaws around the spider's abdomen. Despite the flailing limbs, both worm and meal vanished in a single swift retraction: *shwoop*. The ground puffed a few times, breathing. Spurts of glittering dust rose and fell. Then the clearing was still.

*****

They stopped at a rest station so Li could get some food out of a vending machine. Tetris slouched in the passenger seat, peering out the shattered window. A child walked by, trailing his mother by a couple of steps.

"Mommy," he said, "that man is green."

"That's nice," said the mother, tugging him along.

They ditched the pickup in a riverbed outside Maple, Illinois. The sign at the edge of town said "Population: 157." The first vehicle they came across was an ancient red SUV. It was unlocked. The keys were in the cup holder.

"Small towns," said Li, drumming on the steering wheel as they drove away.

Tetris didn't reply. He was watching the low-slung houses roll by, counting satellite dishes and dogs chained to trees, while he picked buckshot out of his shoulder with a pair of tweezers.

3

The Washington Post's receptionist glared balefully over thick-rimmed glasses.

"I fail to see how painting yourself green constitutes news," he said.

Li laid her palms on the counter. "It's not paint."

"It looks like paint."

"Well, it's not."

Tetris went to peruse the magazines in the waiting area.

Tell him about the photosynthesis, said the forest. *Tell him you healed a shotgun wound in three days.*

"He'll love that," muttered Tetris.

Constrict his throat until the lack of oxygen renders him unconscious?

In the corner, the security guard's stiff posture did little to hide his keen interest in the argument unfolding at the front desk.

"Maybe let us handle this one," said Tetris.

The guard first?

"Trying to get me shot again?"

"What was that?" The receptionist had the phone against his ear and a finger hovering over the dial pad.

"Look," said Tetris, waving a dog-eared men's fashion magazine, "I'm a ranger. I'm bright green. I've got a big story about the thing that turned me green. The least you can do is put me in front of a reporter."

The receptionist flattened his lips. After a moment he returned the phone to its cradle and reached for a bottle of antacid tablets.

"Or," said Li sweetly, "I suppose we could always take our story to the Times."

Five minutes later they were sitting in senior reporter Janice Stacy's office as she tapped a pen against bright pink lips.

"Let me get this straight," said Stacy. "The whole forest is one giant, large, very big alien. From outer space."

"Correct."

"And the government knows."

"Correct."

"And every American ranger has a secret implant in their neck. For, like, mind control, presumably."

"Tracking," said Tetris, "and a kill switch."

"A kill switch."

"To keep us from falling into enemy hands."

"Any other scoops while we're at it? UFOs? Lizard

people?"

Tetris didn't reply.

Stacy scratched at an unsightly residue on the arm of her chair. A few wisps of hair had escaped her bun and were undulating in the air conditioning.

"Where did you obtain this information?"

"The forest told me," said Tetris.

"A giant alien made of trees, from another galaxy, that speaks English."

"I can tell you the exact temperature in any coastal city, anywhere in the world. Right now."

Stacy chewed the end of her pen and watched Li pace the floor-to-ceiling window that served as one of the office's walls. People kept poking their heads out of their cubicles to gawk.

"Mumbai," said Stacy, and turned to her computer.

Tetris tilted his head. "Eighty-six point four degrees Fahrenheit."

The mouse click-clicked. "Osaka."

"Seventy-eight degrees Fahrenheit and raining. It's been raining for the past forty-seven minutes. Year-to-date rainfall is one thousand, two hundred and thirty-three millimeters." He scratched his shoulder absentmindedly. "There are, at this precise moment, one hundred and ninety-three international flights over the world's forests. I can show you the exact position of each one and supply arrival times."

Stacy set the pen on the desk.

"Let me get my editor," she said.

The story ran on the front page. Li and Tetris, who'd spent the night on air mattresses in Stacy's office, emerged the next morning to a horde of reporters, TV vans, and curious passersby. It took an hour to walk the six blocks to the south lawn of the White House, shoving cameras out of their faces the whole way.

Tetris planned on saying a few words to the press when they arrived, but he didn't get a chance. A cadre of suit-clad agents dragged them into the back of an unmarked van.

"You shitheads can't touch us," said Li, relieving a burly hand of its grip around her wrist. The hand's owner yelped.

"You're not under arrest," he said, cradling his fingers and scooting away. "The Secretary of State wants to see you."

Li took an apple out of her pocket and buffed it on her sleeve.

"In that case," she said, biting in with a crunch, "proceed."

The van inched through the mob. Fists rang against the anodized walls.

*****

Toni Davis wasn't sure what color she'd expected him to be. A slight, sickly-green tint, perhaps. But no, he was green with a capital "G," head to toe. Practically Granny Smith-colored.

"Madam Secretary," said Tetris, "you're staring."

"I understand you to be something like an ambassador."

"Sure."

"Well, Mr. Ambassador—"

"Call me Tetris, please, ma'am."

"In America, as in any country, Tetris, we have laws. And while certain action films may have given you ideas to the contrary, we expect ambassadors to abide by those laws. Diplomatic immunity only goes so far."

Tetris looked at Li, who shrugged.

"I'm not sure I understand," he said.

"In the past seventy-two hours, you've publicized highly sensitive state secrets, assaulted a police officer, and stolen three separate motor vehicles."

"Borrowed," said Li.

"Congress is crying treason. Congress wants your little green head."

"Look," said Tetris, "you fuckers put a pod of neurotoxin in my neck. I don't need a lecture on right and wrong. That's wrong."

The subdermals pissed Davis off too. If she'd found out in advance, discontinuing them would have been at the top of her list. Even leaving aside the ethical implications, the program had been guaranteed to set off a scandal whenever the press unearthed it, and the last thing this administration needed was another scandal.

She went with the explanation Cooper had offered. "It's no different from the cyanide pills we used to issue U2 pilots."

"Except those pilots knew in advance," said Li. "They had a choice."

Davis pretended to make a note on her pad.

"I don't think you can blame us for running," said Tetris. "They'd be dissecting me as we speak."

"Of course not," said Davis. "We can't even waterboard you anymore."

"Have you met Cooper?" demanded Li.

"Anyway," said Tetris, "a little transparency never hurt anyone."

"What an unfathomably stupid thing to say," said Davis.

Tetris opened his mouth and closed it again.

"You just told every country with a coastline that a giant alien monster lives next door," said Davis.

"They had to find out sooner or later," said Tetris, "because there's something even bigger on the way."

Davis tugged at an earlobe. There was a painting on the far wall that she looked at when she was thinking. Golden fields rippling in a stiff wind, the mountains in the background jagged and tipped with snow.

"Well?" said Tetris.

Davis clicked her pen and leaned over the desk. "Are you going to explain what that means, Tetris, or are you going to sit there like a vegetable all afternoon?"

*****

28

Vincent Chen was in the Kansas City airport, bumping elbows with a clump of other travelers beneath a small, square television, when he got the call.

"Yes?" he said.

"They're in DC," said Cooper.

"So it seems."

"I assume you're en route?"

"Wheels up in forty-five."

"Roger that."

As Vincent hung up, the station replayed a portion of the footage they'd been broadcasting all morning. The camera zoomed in on a green face, emotionless eyes above a rigid jaw. That, Vincent knew, was not a human being. It was a husk manipulated by a remorseless alien foe. A fat, tendriled parasite wriggled in that hollowed-out skull. Vincent remembered the rabbit with its ragged bite marks. The mouth on the green thing's face looked normal enough, but it was full of teeth designed to tear into living flesh.

"No word yet as to where the so-called Green Ranger was taken, or whether he was telling the truth in his interview with the Washington Post," said the newswoman.

The man next to Vincent turned to a companion. "What's his dick look like, you think?"

The companion considered.

"Definitely some wacko shit," she said. "The image that's coming to mind—and don't judge me, here—is a cucumber with teeth."

"Or is his pelvis straight-up smooth, like an action figure?"

Vincent fought his way out of the crowd and headed for the security line.

4

"Say the words 'tissue sample' one more time," said Li, advancing on a blue-jawed doctor, "and I'll shove those forceps so far up your rear that they'll have to invent a whole new procedure to extract them."

Days of Senate hearings, boardroom briefings, press conferences, and hush-voiced agency interviews. Everyone everywhere asking the same six questions over and over. Nonstop medical appointments, doctors poking and prodding and drawing dizzying amounts of blood. Tetris tugged absentmindedly at the gauze taped over the latest needlehole and wished, above all else, for silence.

"Do I look like—no, *you* listen—tell your boss to come down and talk to me *mano e mano,* capiche? We've seen six doctors today. No more."

There'd been bright points, of course. Dr. Alvarez

blasting around a boardroom table for a rib-flexing hug. The perpetually chastened look on Cooper's face, especially apparent in the presence of Secretary of State Toni Davis.

"-out of my face before I tear it to shreds. That could be Mozart's fucking signature, dude, what will it take for you to understand I don't give a shit?"

"There's no cause for alarm, miss. It's a routine—"

"I'm counting backwards from three, little man, and when I reach one—"

Davis didn't seem like a politician, and of course she wasn't; during the second round of Apollo missions, she'd become both the first African-American and the first woman ever to set foot on the Moon. Tetris had never read her autobiography, *Fuck Your Opinions I'm Doing It Anyway*, but he'd seen display cases full of hardcover copies, her many immaculate smiles gleaming like snowbanks.

At this point it seemed to Tetris that he'd met every member of the United States government except for the President himself, the latter having been called away to attend an international summit in Paris. The summit concerned climate change, but had taken an abrupt turn when Tetris made his existence known. Now the various heads of state were clamoring for more information on the forest, demanding their own ambassadors, and filling the air with fiery rhetoric re: the violation of their coastal borders by the monsters that sometimes spilled out of the verdant depths.

It was a life of continuous noise, without even sleep to interrupt it. When he closed his eyes, he saw the canopy, billowing green.

*****

Ben Jonas was in a store buying clothes for his wife's birthday, which was tomorrow. With everything going on at the White House, he hadn't had time to find a gift online. So here he was, at the mall, his least favorite place, an hour before closing time. Desperate for something, anything, to purchase.

An alarmingly attractive attendant swooped down. "Doing alright?"

"What size would you say the person in this photograph is?" he blurted, shoving his phablet in her well-rouged face.

"Err," she said.

"Aim high and I'm calling her fat," he said grimly. "Aim low and she'll feel like a cow."

"The eternal struggle," agreed the attendant, curls bouncing.

Ben watched her adjust a bra strap. There was something unsettling about her proportions. Alien, almost. He was disgusted. He definitely did not have a boner. How did they get away with wearing such revealing clothing? He was a married man. Old enough to be her father. Okay, he definitely had a boner, it was such a fucked up time to have a boner, what was wrong with him? Everything in his life had been one huge catastrophe since junior prom, when Jace Plaudit pantsed him while he was dancing with Cindy Ducksworth, and the whole school saw his yellowing whitey-tighties with the hole in the rear, and of course he'd had a boner then too—

"Maybe a 12?" suggested the attendant, biting her bountiful lip.

"I'll be taking my business elsewhere, thank you very much," snapped Ben, and trundled out.

*****

You know, said the forest, *if it's more ambassadors they want, we can make more.*

*****

"Come on, man, I brought you out here to have a good time."

"I am having a good time."

"You flinch after every hit."

"It's an awful noise."

"It's an amazing noise. Throaty. You can tell a home run by the sound, you know. It's like a gunshot."

Vincent's shoulder twinged. He drove his thumb deep into the soft tissue and rubbed.

"Ah, shit, my bad," said his brother. "Poor choice of words."

The fans beside Vincent were shirtless and screaming.

Little beads of redolent sweat kept flying off them. They stood and cavorted, shouting, at all times, except between innings, when they sat to gulp beer out of enormous plastic cups.

"You've got to move on eventually," said his brother.

"I have moved on."

A hit, that horrible crack, and the fans went berserk. The all-important white speck vanished in the humming lights and reappeared, plummeting. An outfielder caught it neatly.

"Come on!" shouted Vincent's shirtless neighbor, taking a swing at the air. The other one scowled with his hands behind his buzzcut head.

"It wasn't your fault," said Vincent's brother.

"It wasn't my fault, it wasn't my fault, do you have any idea how many times I've heard you say that?"

"It wasn't, though."

"Look, whose fault it was doesn't change anything. It's meaningless. You think it matters whose fault it was?"

"Don't take it out on me, I'm your last brother, you're—"

"—just wanted to hang out, relax, and not use my fucking brain for five fucking—"

"Hey," shouted the red-faced fan, "can you take your little Communist Party somewhere else?"

"What was that?" said Vincent.

"Vince," warned his brother.

"You heard me, Comrade Ching Chong, I can't hear the damn—"

Another bat crack like a femur snap and Vincent was out of his seat, rising fast, buoyant with electric energy that infused his fists and lifted, at least for a moment, the gray veil over his viscera.

*****

"Go away, Lucia."

Dr. Alvarez slid a finger across the china cabinet. Tsked at the coat of fuzzy dust that accumulated.

"You need a housekeeper, Dave."

"I can't afford a housekeeper," said Dave. He slapped the arm of his wheelchair.

She picked up a photo and wiped it clean. Her own seven-year-old eyes stared back at her. "I could—"

"I don't want your handouts," he said.

"Dave."

"She's long gone, Lucia. Why are you here?"

"I need to check in every once in a while. For my peace of mind."

"No you don't."

She surveyed the graveyard of plastic-wrapped furniture.

"This isn't a way to live," she said.

He turned up the volume. Conservative talking heads traded barbs about national security and the insidious Green Ranger. Dr. Alvarez climbed the stairs, careful not to touch the banister. All the pictures were still on the wall, though some of them were slanted.

Her old room was bare. Even the bed was gone. Where her Marie Curie poster had once hung, the wall was a marginally lighter brown. The floorboards were submerged in gray dust.

Dave was waiting at the bottom of the stairs. A string of spittle connected his chin to his chest. He didn't seem to notice.

"It's your fault, you know," he said.

"What?"

"It's your fault she's dead."

Dr. Alvarez looked at him.

"There was enough for us to live on," he said. "From the settlement. Until you. That's why she went back to work."

The television warbled.

"You think I don't think about that?" she said, harsher than she'd intended.

Dave spat into the dust and wheeled himself away.

*****

Cooper fiddled with an emerald cuff link. Took it out, examined it, put it back.

"Self-defense," said Vincent.

"Bruised trachea, three snapped fingers—"

"He popped me a good one in the eye."

"I can see that. Meanwhile he walked or rather had to be *carted* away, after being hurled down several levels of bleacher, with—"

"He slipped. With great enthusiasm."

"All the scrutiny our department is getting, it seems like a spectacularly bad time for a senior agent to be throwing fists at a ball game."

"They won't be pressing charges."

"I should hope not."

"But. Off the record?"

"My lips are sealed."

"Shithead had it coming."

"That I do not doubt."

*****

"How are you doing, Li?"

Li dunked fries in a paper cup filled with ketchup. "I'm alright, Doc. You?"

"You've been pushing yourself hard."

"I'm going to go ahead and blame your boss for that."

"Cooper means well."

"Neurotoxin pods do not equate, in my mind—"

"Those were an error."

"You're not apologizing, though."

Dr. Alvarez shifted on the red plastic. "I've told you I didn't know about them."

"Sure."

"It was an error. One that I am inclined to believe Cooper regrets."

Their Secret Service agents were posted outside. Stringy clouds whisked across a sky tinged orange by fast-food glass.

"Can't help but notice numerous glances in the direction of the restroom," said Dr. Alvarez.

"He's been in there a long time."

"He's a telepath who spits out buckshot like grape seeds. I'm certain he's fine."

"Again, I'm going to have to blame y'all for the paranoia."

"Everybody always assumes you two are together, don't they?"

The last of Li's soda gurgled through her straw. She sloshed the ice around. "You don't?"

"No."

"We're failing the Bechdel test right now, you know."

"I suppose we'll have to have further conversations, then."

"Do grapes even *have* seeds?"

"Originally, sure. We engineered it out of them."

"If the seeds are gone, how do they grow new grapes?"

Dr. Alvarez opened her mouth, frowned, and closed it.

"Ha! Stumped," said Li.

"I've made a mental note to look into that."

"At last, a factoid the Doctor does not know."

"You would be surprised just how much falls into that bucket."

*****

"What's their plan?"

"He's scheduled to speak to NATO in Paris on the twenty-first. Two days after that, he leads an expedition into the forest. Brings rangers from five or six countries."

"To turn them into plants."

"To turn them into—whatever he is."

"So it's spreading."

"It's six guys. I share your concerns, but it's hardly a pandemic."

"That's the thing about pandemics, Vince: they always start small."

*****

When John Henry, Chief Legal Adviser of the United States Department of State, arrived at his spotless spartan square of an apartment, there was a big evil spider smack in the middle of his marble countertop. Next to the peaches. The peaches he'd been salivating over his entire commute. Fresh, organic, local-ish peaches. So the insecticide spray was out of the question.

He and the spider regarded each other. John Henry made a long and high-pitched sound of distress. His skin was crawling in twelve directions, seeking any avenue off his skeleton. He hated all bugs, but spiders were the worst.

The spider tested the air with a long, waving leg. A brown recluse, perhaps? Known to be aggressive. The vicious serial killer of the arthropod world. Slowly, with great poise, John Henry removed his shoe.

*****

In State Department headquarters, Sasha Montessori and Toni Davis watched the late-night news and dug into freshly delivered pizza.

"How's morale, Sasha?"

"Mmph."

"I wish we could get everyone to see things our way."

"Our?"

"I trust him."

"Can't hurt to be cautious."

"Stationing bombers over the forest goes beyond cautious. Tripling the Coast Guard's budget is blatant opportunism."

"Wouldn't be a real crisis if everyone wasn't trying to turn it to their own advantage."

"JFK have to deal with this shit?"

"You're hardly JFK in this scenario."

Davis caught a strand of half-melted cheese and lifted it to her mouth. "Sometimes, in this administration—"

Sasha grimaced and bit into another slice.

"This is an amazing opportunity," said Davis. "Why are we ruining it with subterfuge and bickering?"

"Because we're human, boss."

"Thank God *it's* not."

5

They were three hours into the flight, thirty thousand feet above the Atlantic Forest, when one of the engines switched from a steady thrum to a keening shriek of metal on metal. It happened with a bang and a shuddering lurch to the left. Smoke whipped past Tetris's window. The plane screamed downward, a steep, spiraling plummet, and he knew in his berserkly-beating heart, as his body rose and strained against the seatbelt, that everything was over. Unique connection to the forest or no, he was going to die.

Five minutes later, he was still very much alive. The noise had not abated. There were fewer screams now, most of the screamers having opted for sobbing into their laps, but the plane's alarms continued to blare, on the off chance that anyone had yet to grasp the gravity of their situation. Furious currents howled against the fuselage, battering it left and right and up and down, but the groaning wings remained attached.

Li had adopted his grim silence, but first she'd been sure to express, matter-of-factly and at great length, her conviction that the plane would come apart when it impacted the canopy. It would, she predicted, fling twisted metal and human debris in all directions.

The wind shrieked vindictively past his window. Everything shook.

I can't tell where you're going to land, said the forest.

Tetris bit his lip and tasted copper.

Get the pilot going in a straight line.

He sucked in a breath and unclicked his seatbelt.

Li yanked his arm.

"I'll be right back," he screamed, tapping the side of his head.

*****

Vincent's reality was a shattering field of glass. Memory-panes flew innumerably by and burst into shards. At some point in the preceding minutes, there had been a very loud noise. The plane had lunged left. Now Cooper was bent in half, praying, and Vincent was crunching the odds of survival. Today would have been his mother's fifty-seventh birthday. Fire and smoke swirled dragonlike past the window.

The green ranger staggered downhill, brushing Vincent on the way by. There was only one reason that someone in this situation would rush in that direction: to reach the cockpit and finish the job.

Vincent caught Tetris at the door, hit him low in the back, and felt the green skull clock the edge of the doorway with a sweet, satisfying *thwock*. The plane tilted even further, and together they slid, Vincent wrapped around the formidable waist, holding on for everything in the universe. Tetris bucked and spun, planting his feet against Vincent's chest, then pushed off as they tobogganed past the lavatories. Vincent grasped at the jackhammering feet. A boot caught him in the teeth.

"Get off!"

Vincent ignored the blood flowing into his eye. A boot hit his face a second time. It seemed harder to dodge these blows when he couldn't hear. It was very likely that his nose was broken.

Fine. He'd wanted to take the saboteur alive, but a couple more blows like that and his consciousness would ebb. He unholstered his pistol and brought it up—

Tetris bucked out of the way, but Vincent still would have adjusted his aim and hit the shot if Cooper hadn't come flying and tackled him. The pistol discharged through the wall, leaving a whistling eraser-tip of vivid blue sky.

The three of them tumbled, all flailing legs and arms, into the C-32's onboard conference room.

Vincent searched for the pistol. It was past Tetris's head, caught on the edge of a chair. Tetris kicked free and reached it first. He ejected the magazine and racked the slide, then flung the empty gun away. Shouted something inaudible.

Vincent struggled, but Cooper was wrapped around him like an octopus. The engines devoured his voice.

"Let him go, Vince," shouted Cooper in his ear.

Vincent kept fighting, but Tetris was already gone.

*****

The plane was crashing. It was going down. There were unspeakable noises coming through the window, and what Ben Jonas wanted to know was where was his oxygen mask? The plane was going down and he couldn't breathe. An oxygen mask was supposed to come out of the ceiling, yellow with an elastic cord, he was supposed to affix his own mask before assisting his neighbor—

The yellow mask would come down and he would put it on and everything would be okay, he would breathe slowly and surely, maybe close his eyes and take a little nap. *Oxygen will be flowing, though the bag may not inflate.* Ben punched the ceiling. Slammed it with both hands. Where was the mask? What had he done?

He sobbed, and the plane fell out of the sky like a dropped sausage, and a green man went down the aisle smelling like a thunderstorm, barging into the cockpit and shutting the door behind him.

*****

The plane came whistling out of the cavernous cloud-swirled sky. Sunlight glinting off the wings would have caught the carnivorous attention of countless canopy denizens, had they not been otherwise occupied.

The thing that had the monsters snapping at one another as they fled was a substance rather like thick green gelatin, which oozed by the megaliter out of the tops of the trees. It formed rolling bubbles and waves above the canopy, blooming upward and dripping through the interlocking branches to splat in heaps on the forest floor.

As the plane approached the rubbery green goop, it extended its landing gear. A pillar of smoke straggled behind it. After a long moment of consideration, the landing gear retracted.

The underside of the plane made contact, skipping lightly across the surface, then gliding, kicking up towering ripples. As it skidded, the plane sank and slowed, until finally it was halfway submerged. It inched forward. It stopped.

Gradually the green substance dissolved and drained away. As it vanished, the plane settled lower, sliding backward, tail inclined toward the ground.

The last part to be swallowed was the cockpit. Then the plane was gone, and the treetops sprang back to their normal positions. A breeze ruffled the canopy as if nothing had happened at all.

*****

Tetris, who'd taken a seat in the forward compartment, unstrapped himself and hurtled into the cockpit. The pilots were busy at their consoles.

"You have to get away from the windows," he said.

Outside, ancient branches twirled into the patchwork sky.

"We're radioing for help," said the co-pilot, glancing at Tetris over a formidably bushy mustache.

"If anything moves," said Tetris, "run."

Then he was headed downhill to the Secretary of State's room. Her Secret Service agents were at the little oval windows, peering into the tangled maze, pistols in firm two-handed grips. Tetris didn't have the heart to tell them that their weapons were basically BB guns.

"Do we have ranger gear on board? Grapple guns? How many grapple guns?"

"Tetris," said Davis, "did you crash my plane?"

"Do I really have to answer that?"

A Secret Service agent yelped and fell on his rear as the room darkened. Smooth yellow flesh slid across the windows. The plane shuddered. Tetris and Davis watched the scales glide slowly by. Creaks from all sides indicated that the snake had wrapped itself around the fuselage.

"We need to get out of the canopy," said Tetris, "or everyone is going to die."

Shouts and the sound of crumpling metal forced him

back toward the cockpit. The anaconda had its mouth over the nose of the plane, serrated teeth-rows and red throat blocking the windows. Inexorably, the mouth closed. The pilots scrambled free, but one of them was a second too slow, and his lower half was caught in a vise of ruined metal.

Where the fuselage had connected to the roof, canopy air poured through. The smell was fecund, sweet, suggestive of clear water. The snake's cold eye appeared in the gap.

The trapped pilot screamed and screamed.

The eye retreated. Moments later, the snake's nose jammed against the gap, black tongue flickering in. It poked and prodded, trying to get at the source of the tantalizing shrieks, driving the plane deeper and deeper into the canopy.

Tetris had the Secretary of State's arm and was rushing her downhill.

"There was equipment for the mission in the cargo hold," Davis said. "But that's on the underside of the plane."

Li met them in the conference room, along with Dr. Alvarez, Cooper, and a glowering Vincent Chen.

"How do I get the cargo hold open?" asked Tetris.

"There's a switch in the cockpit," said Dr. Alvarez.

"Not anymore."

The plane dropped several feet, groaning. Everyone clutched whatever they could get their hands on. The tip of the anaconda's tail flashed past the window.

"You'd have to use a charge, then," said Cooper. "Blow the lock."

"There's C4 in the back closet," said one of the Secret Service agents. Behind sunglasses, his face was almost as green as Tetris's.

Li followed Tetris down the hall. "I'm coming with you."

Passengers cowered in the rear compartment's seats. They seemed as scared of Tetris as they were of the anaconda.

He opened the closet. Bulletproof vests: useless. M4A1 rifles: slightly less useless. He grabbed one of the rifles, slung the strap over his shoulder, and passed Li two more. The C4 was packaged in blocks; he took a backpack and stuffed it full, then made for the emergency exit.

"The monsters can't see me," said Tetris. "I'm invisible to them. You don't need to come."

"Don't use too much," she said, prodding the pack.

She helped him wrench the exit open. A cavalcade of chirps and shrieks tumbled through, along with a rush of over-oxygenated air. Tetris, wishing for climbing picks, leapt the three foot gap to the nearest branch.

Li slammed the door behind him.

The anaconda was wrapped three times around the upper half of the plane, head out of sight as it probed the underside of the fuselage. The pilot's screams had stopped. Above and beside Tetris, an enormous black widow tiptoed closer on vertiginous legs. The red hourglass on its abdomen was as tall as Tetris. The spider reached out—and out, and out—to touch the fuselage, scraping the aluminum tentatively.

Tetris was always amazed by the complexity of parts around a spider's mouth. Fangs, jaws, mouthparts, little frantically rustling pedipalps, and of course the many unblinking eyes...

A second leg probed out beside the first.

Tetris placed a hand on one of the stationary legs. The exoskeleton was cool and hard, like playground infrastructure. He took a chunk of C4 out of his pack, affixed it to the leg, and inserted a remote detonator.

The spider crossed over to the roof.

Hurry up, said the forest.

He turned and climbed the matted vines to the underside of the plane.

The cargo hold already yawned open. Since the plane was rotated slightly onto its left flank, the door pointed downward, and many of the crates and boxes had already come tumbling out. They littered the branches like an abandoned archaeological dig.

As Tetris approached, a millipede the width of a golden retriever poked its armored head out of the hold. Its tiny eyes examined him dumbly. The remains of a crate were stuck like a wreath around its upper segment.

"Get out of here," said Tetris. The millipede ducked from view.

He sighed and flicked the flashlight attached to his rifle.

The cargo hold was long and dark, with a grooved

metal ceiling. The millipede rustled through boxes near the uphill end. Tetris searched the crates beside the door. The fourth box he checked—with a Vertigo Industries logo stenciled on the side—contained six brand-new grapple guns and accompanying harnesses.

He took a grapple gun and nylon webbing and went outside. Sunlight glared through the interlocking leaves. He aimed upward as the millipede came to watch. Its feelers waved.

"I thought they couldn't see me?" said Tetris as he fired. The grapple gun's hook wrapped around a branch a few stories up.

They can see you, said the forest. *It's just that most of them find you tremendously uninteresting.*

Tetris hooked the webbing around the dangling grapple gun and filled it with gear from the boxes.

When he finally ascended, lugging two full packs, the emergency exit door was open. The carpet beyond gleamed with blood, and the seats in the rear cabin were empty.

Tetris threw the packs down, closed the door, and sprinted up the hall with his rifle at the ready, mind crafting worst-case scenarios beyond his wildest nightmares.

6

A three hundred-pound ant was trying to barge through the door to the conference room, antennae shuddering as it threw its weight against the brittle plastic. Tetris stitched a line of fire down its back, but the bullets merely lodged in the exoskeleton.

The ant backed up. It didn't have room to turn, but it craned its neck to look at him. An electric thrill tickled the back of his neck as the sickle-shaped pincers chewed the air. The ant's eyes were huge, expressionless bulbs.

Li kicked the door open, lunged, and slammed a fire extinguisher through the ant's head. Orange fluid plumed in spouts. She jumped back, leaving the canister embedded in the ruined cranium, as the ant spasmed after her. It bounced off the walls and flipped, every leg moving in its own deranged pattern. Finally, with a whine of escaping air, the carnival of limbs fell still.

"That felt great," said Li, extending a hand to help Tetris clamber over the still-twitching carcass.

The room was packed. Tetris recognized several passengers from the rear cabin.

"Whose blood was that?" he asked.

One of the aides retched. Tetris tried not to look at the brownish dribble that followed. He was beginning to understand why the room smelled so awful.

"Some idiot opened the door," said Li. "Couple of bugs ripped him in half and carted him off." She nodded at the extinguished ant. "That one stuck around. Unlucky for him."

"Her," said Dr. Alvarez. "Workers are female."

"Doc. Not the time for entomological quibbles."

Tetris tossed Li the gun. "Only three?"

"They'll be back," said Dr. Alvarez. "They'll bring the whole colony."

Li checked the magazine. "You find grapple guns?"

"Only six."

Li turned to the crowd. "Tetris, Doc, me—who else knows how to use one?"

"I do," said Secretary of State Toni Davis.

Li looked at her. "Come on."

"No," Davis said, "seriously."

"Where'd you learn that?"

"Does it matter?"

Go go go go go go go, said the forest.

"Who else?" snapped Tetris.

Vincent Chen raised his hand. So did one of the Secret Service agents.

"That's six," said Li. "We'll bring the rest of you down in stages."

But the aides were already clamoring forward, pleading for a spot in the first wave. Along the back wall, the pilots stood silently, arms crossed, with a couple other Secret Service agents and Agent Dale Cooper.

"Everybody shut up," said Davis, and the room fell silent. "Jack Dano. Cooper." She scanned the mob. "Evan. Sasha. Kate. Ben. That's the first six. The rest of you will wait your turn."

"I'll stay," said Cooper quietly. He had a bloody tissue pressed to his nose.

"No," said Dr. Alvarez.

Cooper shook his head. Tetris stared at him.

"Somebody's got to hold down the fort," he said. "You can come back for me."

"Cooper," said Jack Dano, "you are mission-critical personnel."

"Alvarez knows everything that I do," said Cooper.

Why is he doing this, wondered the forest.

Cooper's eyes were an impenetrable blue.

"Let's go," said Li.

Tetris shouldered his pack and vaulted the ant. Right

now the only thing to think about was how to move twenty-four people and a dozen packs from the upper canopy to the relative safety of the lowest branches.

"These are full of harnesses," he said, tossing the packs into the arms of the aides closest behind. "I'll be right back."

He peeked out the porthole and swung the emergency exit open, then leaned out for the bundle of gear. After bringing it inside, he disengaged the grapple gun and tossed it to Li as soon as the silver spearhead finished whizzing back into the barrel. Trusting her to sort through the equipment, he leaned out and fired his own grapple gun, then swung down toward the cargo hold.

The millipede was still there. An antenna wiggled a greeting. Tetris gave it a pat on the head, and was surprised to feel it nudge against his leg like a cat. He grabbed the other packs he'd stuffed with equipment and slung them over his shoulders, then hooked the grapple gun to his harness and ascended. As he rose he saw the first of the ants marching along distant branches. The noose was closing.

Inside, everyone had managed to get their harnesses on. One of the aides was too wide to close all the buckles.

"That's not going to hold," said Li, poking him in the stomach.

"Sure it will," he said.

Li looked at Tetris imploringly. "Can't we bring one of the other ones? Someone with a chance?"

"We have to get everybody out of here eventually," said

Davis.

Tetris could tell that Li didn't expect to make a second trip.

"I'll take you," he said to the bureaucrat. "What's your name?"

"Ben," said the man, face shiny with equal parts terror and gratitude.

"Alright, Ben," said Tetris, "do me a favor and put this on."

"What's in there?"

"A shitload of C4," said Tetris. Then, because he couldn't help himself: "Don't drop it." He tossed the bag, and Ben nearly fell over himself trying to keep it off the ground.

"It won't blow up without a detonator," said Dr. Alvarez, scowling at Tetris.

Cooper stood in the hallway. Tetris went over as the rest of the group geared up.

"Here," he said, pressing the M4A1 into Cooper's arms.

"Better that you have it," said Cooper.

"I found a SCAR," said Tetris. "Don't open the door unless you see my face through the window."

"Understood."

Tetris faked a cough. A day ago, he would have listed this man in his five least-favorite people on the planet. Now he got a painful block in his throat just looking at him.

"Why try to be a hero?"

"That's your job," said Cooper, with an attempt at a

jaunty grin.

"I'll be back for you."

"I appreciate that," said Cooper.

Sixty seconds later, Tetris was strapped to a grapple gun and Ben the State Department staffer, flashing through the leaves while the forest chattered into his brainstem. They landed on a wide branch. Tetris detached from Ben, secured the hook anew, and gave the line a good yank to verify its firmness.

When he turned around, Ben was hunched over, head buried in his arms.

"What?" said Tetris.

"I hate heights," warbled Ben.

"Least of your worries, dude. Get up."

He did have to admit that, pressed against the staffer's sweaty flank, he was not looking forward to the weeks they were preparing to spend together. If Ben couldn't meet the group's pace, he'd be blubbering dead weight, a high-caloric snack to draw hungry creatures from all corners of the forest.

He dropped Ben on one of the lower branches and began planning his ascent. The others were coming down after them. Li had just landed slightly higher up, and was berating her staffer about something. The twiggy man's head bobbed vigorously.

The others were descending slower, taking their time, probably scared out of their little civilian skulls. They were doing alright, though, it seemed like, Vincent Chen maybe the slowest of the bunch. Davis was right beneath him, with a woman from the State Department wrapped around her like an inner tube. Davis was doing great. She was almost past the face in the tree. Soon everyone would be safe. Time to head back up, maybe grab some extra gear if there was . . . face in the tree? Face in the tree *there was a giant cat-eyed face in the tree* next to Davis and before Tetris could shout, the mouth yawned, huge yellow teeth unsheathing, the jaw distending and revealing the skin that covered it to be scaly and fluid, the whole gigantic head perched atop a hideous camouflaged body that, as it moved, seemed to tear a section of tree trunk away—

Tetris fired the grapple gun. Vincent swiveled with his M4A1 held one-handed. The burst he unleashed was short, because he couldn't control his spin and swiftly rotated out of view, but it distracted the monstrosity, and the claw slicing through the air merely severed Davis's grapple line instead of tearing her and the staffer in half.

Davis plummeted. The staffer's arms windmilled. Tetris, feeling the grapple gun's hook latch around a branch, leapt into space. The wind flayed the flesh around his eyes, but he kept his tear-streaked gaze on the fast-dropping target, finessing the switch to adjust his altitude as he swung.

Davis and the aide were slowly tilting heels-over-head as they fell, and when Tetris hit them a knee struck him full in the face. Somehow, biting through his tongue, he managed to keep the starstorm at bay long enough to find a firm hold on Davis's harness, clamping through it and around her torso with both arms. In the limb-flailing shuffle, the switch on his grapple gun was depressed again, and they lurched out of the swing into a breakneck fall, until suddenly there was no more line to give.

The jolt was so violent that it broke the connection between Davis's harness and the staffer's. Tetris watched the red-haired woman tumble the final two hundred feet. It took a long time.

Blood from his truncated tongue swirled in his mouth. He hooked his harness to Davis's and pulled her up.

"No," she said.

The lizard-sphinx leaned off the tree far above them and roared, swiping at Vincent, who dangled just out of reach, grimly continuing his descent. Tetris thumbed the switch and whizzed upward. He'd never seen anything like this, never-not-once had he seen a creature resembling this one in any way, but he had a pretty good idea of how to kill it, actually, now that he thought about it. He left Davis on the branch, snatched Ben's pack, and slung it over his shoulder while the staffer gaped and gargled.

Vincent stood on a limb several stories up, trying to line up another shot, his passenger sticking off his back like some kind of shuddering growth. The lizard-sphinx clambered in slow-motion down the trunk of the tree. Tetris fired his grapple gun at the highest branch he could reach, then zipped into the air.

As he ascended, Tetris unloaded his sidearm left-handed to get the beast's attention. It turned his way, saggy mouth groping the air, and as Tetris passed overhead he tossed a brick of C4 down the wide brown throat.

When he hit the detonator, there were two explosions, the second one echoing down from above. Shit.

The spider, said the forest.

"No shibbt," said Tetris, blood clumping in his mouth. The pain was searing. A big chunk of his tongue hung loose. Hopefully that was another thing the forest could fix.

The canopy crashed and thundered. The black widow exploded through, its remaining legs stabbing hopelessly for purchase. It tumbled into empty air, rolling, the red hourglass flashing by, and somehow caught itself around a branch, landing so heavily that its swollen abdomen crunched. Meanwhile, the lizard-sphinx fled up the tree trunk, emitting horrified noises through a hole the size of an ice cream truck in its leathery neck. It spurted a highway of black blood on the bark as it went.

This has produced considerable noise, observed the forest. *I'd advise abandoning the ones in the plane and fleeing while you can.*

Tetris thought of Cooper and grapple-gunned into the canopy. There was still time.

As he reeled in the hook, trying to discern a path upward, Li popped through the foliage and landed on the branch beside him.

"Turn around," she said.

Every word hurt on the way out of his mouth. "Can't leave the otherth."

"They're not coming," said Li.

"Shtill twelve people on that plane."

"And I'm telling you, nobody else is coming."

Tetris fired through a gap in the leaves and rocketed to a vantage point above the plane. It was covered, tail to nose, by wriggling black ants. They swarmed out of the branches and onto the fuselage, while others flowed the opposite way, producing an industrious rustling buzz.

Tetris sat atop a limb and watched.

"Dead?" he asked the forest.

Almost certainly.

Li, who'd followed him up, put a hand on his shoulder.

"We can't stay here," she said.

Tetris thought he saw a human arm protruding from the mouth of one of the faraway ants.

"I'm sorry, Tetris," said Li.

"Thith ith all my fault," he said.

The hand retreated from his shoulder. "No it's not."

Tetris clenched two tight green fists.

"Pfuck," he said. He spat blood over the edge.

"Look, fuckhead," said Li, "I'm trying real hard not to yell, okay? But there are still living human people down there, and every moment you spend here puts their lives in more danger. So can you nut up and get back to work?"

But before Li could protest, he was swinging out over the plane, dropping rapidly, moisture wicking in flimsy strands from the corners of his eyes.

7

Tetris landed on the tip of the wing and waded into the ants. Antennae prodded his torso through his clothes. He fought to the emergency exit and pried at the edges with a climbing pick.

What are you going to do if you find somebody?

He planted a foot on the fuselage and pushed as hard as he could on the pick's handle. The metal groaned.

An ant stepped on his boot, lancing him through the thick leather. Tetris threw his whole weight against the pick. The door swung open of its own accord, and he stumbled backwards, tossed by a swell of ants. He glimpsed wet human eyes and a gasping mouth, and then everything vanished under a thousand thrashing legs.

The footfalls stabbed him from all sides, and he rolled, covering his face with his arms. Trampled to death by ants. How stupid was that? What had he expected? He tried striking out, but the ants didn't even seem to know he was there.

Then something ignited above him, the heat crackling away all the moisture in the air, leaving a sucking desert emptiness. Drops of molten liquid burned holes in his skin. The view through his closed eyelids was searing orange-red. He rolled away as his lips sizzled, the weight of the ants gone as if swept by a great gust of wind.

Li stood before him, holding aloft the smoking nozzle of a flamethrower.

"How many times do I have to save you before you start listening to me?"

"Where—how -"

She kicked him in the shin. "One of the crates. C'mon."

He stumbled to his feet as Li stowed the nozzle on the fuel-canister backpack.

"We're not jusht leaving," said Tetris, mouth thick with blood.

"Do you have a brain disease?"

Flames licked hungrily from the emergency exit. The interior was an inferno packed with writhing ants.

"There was a person there," said Tetris.

"Emphasis on 'was.'"

Ants streamed out of the flames, roasting in their exoskeletons, tumbling off the wing and vanishing. Tetris gave the plane one last look and secured his grapple line. Li was already descending. He burst through the leaves after her.

The black widow had deflated. Its remaining legs were curled in final agony. Trees like temple columns converged on a mess of roiling vegetation far below. The other survivors were scattered across the branches, enraptured by the flaming ants plummeting out of the canopy like a hailstorm from Hell.

As Tetris and Li rappelled the final fifty feet, a flesh wasp the size of a small helicopter buzzed slow-motion around a trunk. It headed toward Toni Davis and Ben. Tetris drew the SCAR from its sling as the wasp flashed between him and the others, but he didn't dare fire. He thumbed the grapple gun and landed heavily on the nearest branch. As he reeled in the line, the wasp dove for Ben. Through the silver fan of wings, Tetris saw the staffer recoil and pitch over the edge.

The flesh wasp chased the tumbling bureaucrat, caught him out of the air, and carried him off, weaving between trees. The giant stinger pierced flesh, and Tetris stopped watching. He landed beside Davis.

"We're leaving," he said, spitting blood. He wondered if he was supposed to feel guilty for having hoped the wasp would take Ben and not Davis.

Dr. Alvarez swung away to the east. The others followed. Davis, hooked to Tetris's harness, wore one pack and carried another. With so much weight, they bowled through the air like a wrecking ball. Tetris turned his face aside as they smashed into the next tree, but the bark tore his cheek open. He found purchase with a climbing pick and hauled them around to the nearest limb, shoulders screaming from the exertion.

Behind them, the ant-swarmed jetliner came sliding through the leaves. Flames spurted out of the wings and fuselage as the plane fell. When it hit the forest floor, it smashed straight through and into the howling depths.

Tetris and Davis joined the others in flight.

*****

They nursed sore joints and oozing gashes in a ragged circle on the forest floor. Insects buzzed and skirled, eliciting nervous swats. Li sat cross-legged against a tree and examined the flamethrower for damage. There was only enough fluid left for another few spouts. When it ran out she'd take her SCAR back from the twiggy government aide she'd entrusted it with. Speaking of which:

"Brand," she said, "if you don't stop pointing your weapon at people, I'm going to punt you into a ravine."

Evan Brand, a forty-something tetherball-post of a man, sheepishly stowed the SCAR in its sling across his back. He blinked through thick glasses and tried a tentative smile. She didn't smile back.

"We're five hundred miles from the coast," said Tetris. "That's at least four weeks, if we make good time."

Li sighted down the flamethrower nozzle. "We won't."

"Six weeks is a better guess," admitted Tetris.

"Can we survive that long?" asked Davis. Her eyes were icepick-sharp through the grime.

Tetris examined a bloody scrape on his shoulder. "The

forest can help with food and water. But it's not that simple. Our group's too large."

"Then we split up," said Davis.

"Suicide," said Li.

"Tetris could take one group," said Dr. Alvarez. "You and I could take the other."

Li tested her hunting knife's edge on her finger. "You're in no position to be guiding anyone."

"I've been training, studying—"

The knife slammed back into its sheath. "The answer is no, Doc."

Dr. Alvarez yanked her pack straps and turned away.

"The forest has a suggestion," said Tetris, "but you're not going to like it."

Jack Dano, Vincent Chen, and the Secret Service agent wore identical scowls. Their black suits, with slacks stuffed into combat boots, were riddled with gruesome tears. Those clothes would be soon be ribbons, if their owners weren't too.

"There's a neurological center two hundred miles from here," said Tetris. "It's out of the way, but if we make it, the forest could turn you into conduits like me. Then we'd be invisible."

"Absolutely not," said Jack Dano, tugging his tie knot.

Vincent drew his pistol. Li released the flamethrower and rose.

"Drop it," she said, her own pistol gliding out of its holster.

"I knew this was a trap," said Vincent.

"Drop the gun, dipshit," said Li, sighting on his forehead.

Tetris approached until Vincent's pistol was three inches from his eye.

"Think very carefully about what happens after you pull that trigger," he said.

Vincent stared back without flinching.

"Weapons down," said Davis. She spoke quietly, but the force of the command was so great that Li lowered her pistol at once. Vincent followed suit. Jack Dano tore his tie off, balled it up, and threw it into the undergrowth.

Davis glared at each of them in turn.

"No more," she said, the softness of her voice failing to conceal its titanium edge. "No more of this. Do you understand?"

Vincent looked at Tetris.

"Do you understand?" repeated Davis.

"Yes," said Vincent.

"Yes, ma'am," said Li. She holstered her pistol, unable to stymie a grin.

"Tetris," said Davis, "how much time would this detour add?"

Tetris inclined his head, listening. "About a week."

"Li," said Davis, "if we take the direct route, what's your professional opinion of the likelihood that everyone survives?"

"Negligible."

"Come on."

"We left the plane with twelve, and we're already down to ten. What's that tell you?"

"What about the forest's plan? What's that do to our odds?"

"Still two hundred miles to cross," said Li. "I'm sorry, but unless we're extremely lucky, and everybody listens to exactly what Tetris and I say, which I doubt is going to happen, people are going to die."

"Christ Almighty," said Evan Brand, wiping his glasses on his shirt, which served only to smudge them more.

"I do think Tetris's plan is your best chance," said Li.

Tetris seemed to have forgotten they were there. He was tracing lines on his palm, mouthing words they couldn't hear. The faces around the circle were a palette of misery. Li leaned on her right leg, stretching. No point in thinking about anything except the path directly in front of her.

Davis scratched behind her ear. "Who here would become a conduit if the opportunity arose?"

The three staffers raised their hands, along with Dr. Alvarez. After a moment, Davis put her own hand up.

"All that talk," she said to Li, "and you aren't willing to do it yourself?"

"I'm not the one who needs the help," said Li.

"What about you three?"

"No thank you, Madam Secretary," said Jack Dano. Vincent and the agent grunted agreement.

"We'll take the detour," said Davis. "Lead the way."

8

Douglas "Hollywood" Douglas walked along the shore in the evenings, hands in his pockets, gazing only occasionally into the blue-black depths. The Coast Guard had stopped him frequently at first, but now his strolls went largely unmolested. He did technically have clearance to be there, and anyway their job was more to keep things in than out.

He walked outside the floodlights' yellow humps, shrouded, silent, interfacing with the breeze.

A sentient forest was no surprise. He'd felt the truth congeal days after laying eyes on the first obelisk. Even before the dreams. He spat, unsure if he envied Tetris or pitied him.

Most of the dreams had involved his mother. She'd looked avian enough in real life, but in the dreams she'd had feathers sticking off her body at crazy angles, the points jammed bloody under her skin. Completing the nightmare were bulging black eyes and a beakish mouth without teeth. She never formed words, just moved her mouth and screamed, and if he struck out she exploded into polygonal shards, then solidified alternately into a towering bull, a Tyrannosaur, or an aquatic creature of unfathomable bulk. Shadow-black, spouting blood from sewer-drain apertures, howling nonsense words, the visions chased him into consciousness again and again, until one day they simply ceased.

This particular chapter of his altogether dissatisfying past was what Hollywood happened to be mulling over, chewing his lip, at the exact moment when three furtive shapes darted through the floodlights and into the forest ahead.

He pursued on the long, tan, muscular legs that were his proudest possession. People like this were all over the news since Tetris made his announcement. Deluded by pseudo-religious reverence, something like three thousand nutjobs embarked on an ill-fated pilgrimage into the forest every day. (Multitudinous public service announcements, in which Tetris himself had stated bluntly that the forest was not accepting applications, had done nothing to dissuade the legions of faithful.)

The would-be explorers had a considerable head start. Hollywood fought through the brush, following the erratic dance of their flashlight, ducking whenever a thorny branch leapt out to stab him. He was afraid to shout, and the idiots couldn't hear him over their own much clumsier footsteps, so they only noticed his presence when he finally clapped a hand on one man's shoulder.

The man screamed, wriggled out of the grip, and stumbled into a thicket of razorgrass. Then screamed even more, of course, thanks to the lacerations that immediately resulted...

"Shut the fuck up," hissed Hollywood, but it was too late.

As the leader of the group turned, the beam of his upward-swinging floodlight illuminated, ever so briefly, an image soon to be tattooed across Hollywood's brainpan: a wedge-headed titan framed between the trees, legs wider than the trunks, with an acromegalic jaw several stories tall. A fusillade of horns erupted from the beast's smooth skin with a squelch-pop like ten thousand shovels pulled out of the mud at once. The creature's breath bloomed, a green-tinged miasma, forty-five feet above the forest floor.

The sight was cut short when the expedition's leader pointed his light square in Hollywood's eyes. Hollywood only had time to utter the "G" in "Get back" when the creature unleashed a roar so astounding in volume that it literally knocked them all off their feet.

As he scrambled up and began to run, Hollywood cursed the lurid purple splotches left by the flashlight. He felt for obstacles as he went, twice stumbling on the rough ground and only barely managing to right himself.

He could feel someone else behind him, but it wasn't the man with the flashlight. The flashlight was gone, likely crushed alongside its unfortunate owner. The last of the undergrowth whipped by, and then Hollywood was out onto open ground.

The beast followed, submandibular tusks splintering through the outermost trees. Hollywood shouted, waved his arms, and ran, refusing to look back. Then came the massive percussive coughing of the Coast Guard howitzers, the shriek of their shells, and the candent flare of enormous muzzles. He lowered his head, motoring up the steep slope even as his quads begged for relief.

The earth gave its hardest quake yet, and for a moment he thought the beast had somehow leapt and landed close behind him, but when he glanced back its bulk was settling into the ground, gray flesh pockmarked by the great steel guns. Horns retracted and thrust forth and retracted again, a deranged steampunk factory of flesh and bone.

The creature knelt, bellowing, and then a missile streaked in and engulfed the lower portion of its skull in a dodecahedron of flame. The base of the jaw hit the ground a full two seconds before the rest of the head.

What Hollywood found himself thinking about, as the monster's veins proved to course with flammable blood, igniting a conflagration with an aroma not unlike that of a pig on a spit, was not the question of why such an immense creature had been prowling so close to the periphery, nor the fate of the men who had failed to escape, but the shimmering path to pecuniary success that had unfolded before him. He felt the way Rockefeller must have felt, seeing oil for the very first time. His face stretched in what he could hardly have been expected to realize was a predatory leer at the sniveling man who'd escaped alongside him.

"You know," he said, "if you're going to attempt something as ill-advised as an jaunt into the forest, the least you could do is hire a good guide."

He walked off whistling as the carcass popped and crackled behind him, pillars of sparks rising like red gods into the starless sky.

9

From the moment she carried him out of the plane, Evan Brand was in love with Lindsey Li. She reminded him of a girlfriend he'd had back in college. Two decades (had it really been that long?) hadn't dulled memories of that girl, who had been slight and pretty and had covered her mouth when she laughed despite a set of teeth that made Evan's feel yellow and crooked.

Actually, come to think of it, Li was a lot taller than that girl, and nowhere near as slender. Not overweight, just... sturdy. Li's muscles didn't bulge, but when you were pressed against her, as he had a chance to be every time they grapple-gunned in or out of the trees, you couldn't help but notice that her body was made of iron. And her hands... she could catch a cannonball with those hands.

When she laughed, she just plain laughed—no mouth-covering necessary.

So what was it about Li that reminded him of his college girlfriend? Surely it wasn't just that she was Asian. She wasn't even the same kind of Asian. He dimly remembered that his college girlfriend had been either Korean or Japanese, or perhaps (but probably not) Thai, and "Li" was (he was pretty sure) a Chinese name. Li's hair was extremely short, and she scowled a lot, which the college girlfriend had never done, scowling having perhaps been groomed out of her by a strict Korean/Japanese/Thai upbringing, although Evan believed he'd noticed Li scowling a bit less at him, recently, which was as a promising sign.

Evan was not a racist. He worked for an African-American Secretary of State, for Christ's sake! Some of his closest friends were non-white colors, and anyway he'd voted for Obama in both 2008 and 2012. Surely there was some other commonality between Li and his college girlfriend, something subtle, that was causing him to feel this way.

He stood before a wall of vegetation with his zipper down—consumed, as his urine steamed on the leaves, by this same old internal debate—when the vegetation lifted away to reveal a ten-foot-tall, corpulent blue toad, the foot of which Evan had, up until this very moment of prostate-shriveling fear, been piddling upon.

The toad peered down and produced a dissatisfied noise somewhere in the ballpark of "*Glorp*."

Evan shrieked and turned to flee, yanking frantically

on his zipper, only to run smack into Lindsey Li.

"It won't hurt you," she said, grinning. "Just don't touch it."

"Glorp," the toad agreed.

"Oh my God, no, no no no," said Evan, scampering around her in as dignified a manner as possible.

And that was the exactly the problem, there, and the reason that his pining for Li would never go anywhere: she would never take him seriously. He was aware of his ridiculous appearance—his tattered suit pants tucked into combat boots two sizes too large, his glasses perpetually grimed over now that he no longer had anything dirt-free to clean them with, his shoulders the narrowest in a group that included four women—but even more damaging than that was his incompetence, his audible cowardice, and his overall net-negative impact on their likelihood of survival.

He had to do something to prove himself. But whenever the opportunity arose, his lizard brain took over and sent him running for cover.

The explorers had divided themselves into factions, with Jack Dano, Vincent Chen, and the Secret Service agent unifying around their distrust of Tetris, while Li and Dr. Alvarez set themselves diametrically opposed, and the others wavered somewhere in the middle. Sometimes, when an argument broke out, Evan would try to take Li's side, but for some reason this seemed to piss her off even more. E.g.:

"I'm not eating this shit," said the Secret Service agent, whose name was Clint, as he hefted a pair of the tubers the forest had recommended. "How do I know these aren't full of mind-control chemicals? Let's kill an animal and eat that."

Li took a defiant bite out of her own tuber. "How do you plan to cook an animal, genius? Think even if you can get forest wood to burn, you can roast something without the smell drawing every predator in five miles?"

"I think the roots taste great," lied Evan as he tried to choke a mouthful down. "A complex, buttery flavor with nutty undertones."

Li fixed him in one of her disemboweling glares.

"Joke all you want," she said, "but it's better than going hungry."

"I wasn't—it wasn't supposed to be—"

"You're all ungrateful shitheads," said Li, and went to check on Tetris.

*****

Night falling, the sound of crickets and things much larger than crickets, a gully-rustle of hidden canopy. John Henry wormed deeper into his sleeping bag. The leaves made a sound not unlike rainfall when a breeze went through.

The ferocious female ranger was untying her boots on the branch beside him.

"What's your name?" he asked.

"Lindsey Li. You?"

"John Henry."

"What do you do, John Henry?

"I head the United States Department of State Office of the Legal Adviser."

"You said 'State' twice."

"Yeah, that's a recurring issue. We're all employees of the United States Department of State, so."

"Not all of us."

"Evan Brand, Sasha Montessori over there... that's it, now, I guess."

"What's on your mind?"

He tightened the drawstring, shivering. "I shouldn't be here."

"None of us are particularly happy about this situation."

"No, I mean, the Secretary didn't call my name at first. She called Cooper."

Li scraped mud off her boots with a knife, a pen light held between her teeth.

"I don't know why he passed," said John Henry. "But I suppose I should be grateful."

"Let me ask you something," said Li, stowing her light and affixing the boots to her pack. "Do you think Dale Cooper was a good person?"

He thought about it. "No better than the rest of us, I suppose."

"Then why do you think he gave up his spot?"

Someone stifled a cough in the darkness.

"I imagine I'll spend the rest of my life trying to figure

that one out," he said.

*****

"Can I trust her, Lucia?"

Dr. Alvarez crunched on a tuber. "Madam Secretary—"

"For the last time, Doctor, call me Toni, or I swear to God—"

"Toni, the young rangerette is good-hearted, as much as she tries to disguise it. But she's also the most fiercely loyal person I think I've ever met."

"To her boyfriend."

"He is absolutely not her boyfriend. That I can relay with zero reservations whatsoever."

"But she'd side with him."

"Over anyone."

"Her behavior seems erratic."

"Vincent's behavior is erratic. The forest is erratic. There is nothing—and I mean nothing, Madam Secretary—erratic about Lindsey Li."

*****

It was four in the afternoon, they were stopped before a fungal wall, and the starfish were singing. Thousands of them suspended in the orange murk. Evan Brand ran his tongue over his teeth, the chipped canine with its inadequate cap. He had a rash on both arms and across his chest like a bandolier. Zits were popping out all over his face. He could feel them. There was dirt everywhere, a little less thick where he'd been scratching his rash. His white dress shirt with its neat blue grid pattern was ripped in several places and hanging away from his body. Through the gaps you could see his skin. Insects flew buzzing through the gaps and he swatted them idly, with the air of a practiced and fastidious executioner. Even his eyes itched. His glasses were nebulaic with grease and dirt. He was desperate for a chance to service himself, but of course there was never a free moment, always someone a few feet from him, even at night.

Something evolutionary seemed amiss, there, that he could be distracted from the grave business of survival by a reproductive impulse. His feet in their ill-fitting combat boots were chafed and bleeding in five or six places. His socks were yellow with sweat, brown with dirt, darker brown with dried blood, and stiff as tree bark all over. Some kind of pollen had accumulated in his hair, freezing it like a paintbrush crusted with dried honey.

He was far past dirty, to a plane of existence where his skin could have been replaced by soil and he wouldn't have noticed. The night before, he'd dreamed that mushrooms grew out of his skin, and when he pulled them off, great chunks of flesh came with. Tiny fungi dotted the walls of the weeping wounds.

*****

"You know what needs to be done," said the Secret

Service agent.

Vincent slashed at some ferns with his machete. "Take those sunglasses off. You look like a fucking idiot."

"They're prescription sunglasses, man, I can't—"

"Seriously?"

"Either everything's dark or it's blurry, okay? I pick dark."

"I'm out here with Ray Charles watching my god damn back—"

"It's not just him. Push comes to shove, we have to ice her too."

"Ice, huh? That's your chosen euphemism?"

"Otherwise she'll kill us all, man. You've seen what she can do."

"I know, okay? I know."

*****

Tetris was up in the canopy catching some sunlight when Vincent remarked to Li that the green ranger sure spent a lot of time skulking around behind their backs. Evan Brand ignored the shouting match that ensued, peering at the shifting landscape of speckled leaves. All he wanted was a slice of sky.

When Tetris came zipping out of the canopy, waving his arms, it was Evan who saw him first, which is why he was the only one with a gun out when the monitor lizard hurtled into the clearing. The lizard's blunt gray snout weaved toward Li, tongue flicking, and Evan reacted without thinking, firing wildly as he dove to shove her out of the way.

The lizard flinched under the barrage of bullets, but Evan's magazine emptied far too quickly, and then there was nothing to stop the creature from knocking him on his back. The useless SCAR rebounded from his fingers. He tried to kick as the red-ridged depths yawned before him, but with a sound like all the winds in the world colliding, the teeth closed around him at the waist. With a gentle tug, the lizard separated Evan's lower half from the rest of him. Evan watched the beast toss its head back and swallow his legs.

A jet of fire struck the creature's head. It turned and received a blast of napalm full in the face, and then it was gone, the tip of its tail flashing briefly across Evan's field of view.

He looked at the canopy. The leaves still rustled the same way, whispering over each other, oblivious. Somehow that made him feel like everything was going to be alright.

Li came into view with the flamethrower nozzle in her hand. She was saying something, but he couldn't hear anything over the wind. He looked at her and smiled.

His last thought, as the whiteness swallowed him up and carried him away, was that the reason she reminded him of his college girlfriend was the face she was making right now: the face she made when she was puzzled, squinting with just one eye and biting the corner of her lip.

10

"Don McCarthy has no diplomatic experience, zilcho name recognition, and reptilian mannerisms that would alarm all but my most delusional supporters. What on Earth makes you think he'd be a passable replacement for the most popular Secretary of State in history?"

"Sir, he's the director of the Coast Guard. You've heard what they're saying: 'the President is soft on the forest, the President let the forest murder Toni Davis—'"

"I could go out there and announce that bears shit in the woods and the House would pass a bill claiming the opposite within twenty-four hours."

"Reelection is almost upon us, sir, and the forest is shaping up to be the number one issue."

"That's your rationale? *'It's the forest, stupid?'*"

"Shouldn't you be building a case for why you're the one to deal with it?"

*****

"Douglas."

"Zachary."

"..."

"May I come in?"

"You are aware that it's three o'clock in the morning?"

"So?"

"So I'm going back to bed. Goodbye, good night, good riddance, au revoir."

"Hey!"

"Get your foot out of the door. Just because you've got more legs doesn't mean I can't kick your ass."

"Measure your words, Zip. I'm on a mission of peace."

"Peace? Man, all I've got is peace. My life is unrelenting peace. Move your foot and come back in the morning."

"I've got a job offer for you, dude."

"I don't need a job. I've got a government pension and a dumpsterload of savings."

"Zip, I am not a brilliant man. I'll admit it."

"That's brave of you."

"I am not a smart man. But even I am not dumb enough—Ow, dude, stop it! What's that made of? Adamantium?"

"Rubber tip. The pole's carbon fiber, though. Space-age crutches. I've got a second one for when I really want to move."

"As I was saying: I am not dumb enough to believe for one millisecond that you are the least bit satisfied with the legless life you're living. Nobody goes happily from ranger to invalid unless they've lost a few lobes along the way."

"I'm fucking thrilled, Hollywood. Life is thrilling. You know I've been learning other languages? Spanish, French, Mandarin."

"You know, I'm about to have a lot of time on my hands, too."

"Mhhmm."

"Rangers are going the way of the Australopithecus, thanks to your buds. May they rest in peace."

"I'm not convinced they're dead."

"Their plane crashed in the forest."

"Have you met them?"

"Anyway I'm not here to talk about them, I'm here to talk about us."

"There's no 'us.' You know I've got a ferocious animal, right? Bite through your Achilles if I say the word. Chomper! C'mere."

"I'm starting a company."

"Oh no. No no no."

"Forestourism, Zip. I don't know why nobody's thought of it before."

"I'm not going back out there."

"That's not what I want. I want you to train these morons. Like Rivers did for us."

"Then ask Rivers."

"I did. He told me to fuck off."

"Shocking."

"You can have ten percent, dude."

"Ten?"

"Fifteen."

"Fifty and I'll consider it."

"All due respect, bud, but your job's the easy one."

"Twenty-five."

"Eighteen point seven five. Final offer."

"..."

"And you gotta let me crash at your place tonight."

"..."

"Your fearsome hound appears to have forgotten how to retract his tongue."

"Fine. *Fine*. You can sleep on the couch."

*****

Repelling the monitor lizard used up the last of the flamethrower ammo. Li dumped the empty weapon next to Evan's body. He'd half-closed his eyes at the last moment, and slivers of white peeked between his lids. His head lolled when she lifted him up to get the blood-sodden pack off.

Behind her, John Henry whispered a prayer under his breath, raking his beard with quick strokes of a long-fingered hand.

"I'm next, aren't I?" he said.

"Nobody's next," said Li. "We shouldn't have been

shouting."

Vincent kicked the dirt and refused to look in Evan's direction.

"Get moving," Li barked. "We can't stay here."

Tetris crouched beside the body, muttering and stabbing his finger in the dirt. He was growing. Bulking up, muscles bulging in places she hadn't noticed before, but also growing taller. She could tell by the widening gap between the ends of his sleeves and his hands. She just hoped it was only his body that was changing, and not his mind.

Tetris closed Evan's eyelids with a monstrous green hand.

"Let's go," he said, glancing disinterestedly across her face.

She almost missed the yearning-puppy looks.

*****

"What's Montessori's role?" asked Li, cracking open a tuber. Toni Davis was the only non-ranger who exhibited zero fear of heights. When they were up in the branches, everyone else stayed strapped in, casting nervous glances at the hungry void. Davis didn't seem to care.

"She's the Executive Secretary," said Davis. A gash above her left eye was beginning to scab over. Like the others, she'd sawed her hair short with a combat knife, and rough edges protruded spikily from her skull.

Li took another flavorless bite. "I thought you were the

Secretary."

"She's the director of my Executive Secretariat."

"That clears it up, huh?"

"It's convoluted. I don't blame you for your confusion."

"She's a secretary's secretary."

"And yet she outranks everybody here but me."

"Even Dano?"

"Interdepartmental comparisons get a touch byzantine."

"She never says a word, I've noticed."

"That's because she's mute."

"What?"

"Ha! Got you. No, she's just taciturn."

"Holy shit, Madam Secretary—"

"This 'Madam Secretary' business has got to stop."

Li scratched her neck. "Yes, ma'am."

"Even ma'am is pushing your luck."

"What can I say? I'm an adrenaline junkie."

Li's eyes never stopped moving, flitting across the forest floor, idly checking for the next thing that would try to eat them. It would be dark soon. Elsewhere in the branches, the others talked in voices too quiet to make out, a reassuring tumble of human sound.

"Nah," said Davis.

"Excuse me?"

"You don't have this job because you're an adrenaline junkie. You're something else."

"What's your hypothesis?"

"I don't know you well enough to make one. But I know it's not that."

*****

"I wanted to be a ranger when I was small," said Sasha Montessori, screwing bolts into the branch to secure her sleeping bag.

"What changed?" asked Dr. Alvarez, squinting across the gap at Li and Toni Davis.

"Everybody told me it was a stupid idea."

"Was it?"

"Maybe."

"You made out alright."

"I did."

Dr. Alvarez brushed dirt off her rifle. "Seems unlike you to heed the haters, though."

"It was the last time I ever did."

*****

"When this is over," said Davis, "I want you to come work for me."

Li stopped chewing. "Hwaa?"

"You heard me."

"Sorry, ma'am, but I'm not cut out for Washington."

"You'd be surprised."

"I belong out here."

"You don't seem to be enjoying it much."

"Might have something to do with the company."

"Vincent and Dano get on your nerves. But the rest of

us?"

"I've got a lot of respect for you, Madam ... ahem, Toni. But right now you're a liability."

A dark shape crashed through the undergrowth far below, pursued by a larger, darker shape with far more legs.

"Anyway," said Li. "You're not in a position to offer me anything. They've probably already given your job away."

"Why did you become a ranger, Li?"

"Same reason you became an astronaut."

Davis shook her head. "I'm never going to escape that book."

"*Fuck Your Opinions, I'm Doing It Anyway*," intoned Li.

"You wouldn't believe how the publisher screamed when I told him I wanted to put the F-word on the cover."

"It's the 21st century. Why do people still care?"

"I guess it makes them uncomfortable, imagining the acts the words describe."

"Tough shit."

"Well. If there's one thing I learned as Secretary of State, it's that common courtesy goes a long way."

"And that's why I couldn't be a politician," said Li.

"You wouldn't have to be a politician to work for me."

Li squinted. The dusk made it hard to discern exactly which emotions were battling it out on Davis's face.

"Why do you even like me?" asked Li. "I've been nothing but rude to you and everyone else. Not that I regret it. I just don't understand how you get from there to here."

"You're blunt. Honest. Smart, and careful. To me it seems like your talents are wasted in your current profession."

"I'm good at my job."

"I know."

A side effect of the grime was an itchiness that rose and fell when you least expected it. Li scratched her legs just above her stiff socks. The skin was raw and papery, but it felt too good to stop.

"There's nothing you need that I could do," she said.

Davis turned her sidearm in her hands and stared down the barrel. Li refrained from snapping about the danger of pointing a gun at yourself. After a while Davis stowed it and released the kind of sigh that, in Li's experience, always preceded a long story.

"When I was young, I did some tremendously stupid things," said Davis. "One of those things resulted in me getting pregnant."

This, Li knew, had not been mentioned in the memoir.

"Becoming a teenage mother would have torpedoed all my plans. No chance of college, or becoming an astronaut. But my parents were religious. They wanted me to keep the baby."

"But you didn't," said Li.

"I went back and forth," said Davis. "What pissed me off was that the father of the child got to go on with his life. For him it was a blip. A speed bump. He could cruise forward and achieve everything he wanted, as long as he made the child support payments. But for me—"

"You had the abortion?"

"I was on my way to the clinic," said Davis, "when I felt something. A kick, except that that was impossible, it was way too early. But a movement. Something. Like it—like she—was saying *stop*. And I decided that I couldn't do it. I told my mom to turn around and drive me home. I'd have the baby. I certainly would never judge another woman for the choice she made. But for me, right then, right there... I just couldn't do it."

Li could barely see Davis's face, now, no matter how she strained.

"You had the baby," she said.

"Two weeks later, I miscarried."

"Oh my God."

"This is the awful part, though: the first thing I felt, when I realized what had happened, wasn't horror. It was pure electric relief. And even though the horror set in afterward, the guilt for that initial moment has never gone away."

"I'm so sorry," said Li.

"Anyway, the reason I bring it up," said Davis, shifting on the branch, "is that she'd be about your age. So I guess you remind me of her. Of what she might have grown up to be."

The leaves whispered over one another, innumerable in perfect darkness.

"How do you know it was a girl?" asked Li.

"Good night, Li," said Davis, unzipping her sleeping bag.

11

The next time Vincent started an argument, Tetris, at this point well over six feet tall, walked up and struck him on the chin. Vincent fell like an unmoored elevator. Tetris crashed down close behind. When the agent pulled his gun, Tetris plucked it from his hand and socked him another one in the jaw.

"I could kill you," observed Tetris.

"Stand down," said Toni Davis.

"Get off him, T," said Li, SCAR pointed at nothing in particular. Her eyes were glued to Jack Dano and the Secret Service agent.

Tetris loomed over Vincent, green fists twitching.

"Please, Tetris," said Dr. Alvarez.

Blood trickled from Vincent's split lip. "Fuck you," he said, and spat.

"I'm trying to save you," said Tetris, oblivious to the blood speckling his face.

"Like you saved Cooper?"

Tetris hit him again. Vincent's head snapped back like a yo-yo. Davis rushed in and shoved Tetris aside. Tried to, at least. Tetris examined her face, then stepped abruptly away. The pistol fell from his fingers. He stalked into the undergrowth, shrugging out of his grapple gun and harness as he went.

"Good riddance," said Jack Dano.

"He'll be back," said Li.

Vincent spat red-black phlegm.

"Your boyfriend is a psychopath," he said. "We'll be better off without him."

"Are you sure he's coming back?" asked Sasha Montessori.

"He'll come back," said Li, gathering up the gear he'd dropped.

They waited all afternoon. When they made camp for the evening, Tetris was nowhere to be found. Li's relief that he'd taken some time to cool off turned to fury as she imagined him sulking in a tree somewhere.

"Do we go on without him?" asked Davis the next morning.

Li hefted the SCAR.

"I'm sure he's just out of sight," said Dr. Alvarez.

Li wanted to shout something into the undergrowth—"Hey shithead, get over yourself"—but making that much noise was irresponsible. She'd never seen him do anything this petulant. Maybe the forest was getting to him.

By lunch there was still no sign of him.

"Let's go," said Li. "He'll catch up."

It was impossible to imagine him abandoning them. And yet... two days passed as they trudged along in the general direction they'd been headed, and Tetris never showed himself.

"It's time to stop going north," said Vincent. "We've got to go east, toward the coast."

"We'll never make it," said Li.

"We'll never find the anomaly without him anyway," said Dr. Alvarez.

A pillbug snuffled in the weeds. Sasha Montessori eyed it with quiet fascination. John Henry stood as far away from the creature as possible.

"East it is," said Li, shouldering her pack.

She figured that straying off the path might lure Tetris out of his pout. Except it didn't. With each passing hour, Li grew angrier at him, and simultaneously more worried. The whole situation was bizarre. There was no explanation for his behavior. Tetris would never have abandoned them like this. Which meant that he was no longer Tetris.

One afternoon, as they passed an oblong meadow packed with brownish-yellow butter mushrooms, a scorpion burst out of the undergrowth and hurtled toward them, pincers raised.

"Go!" shouted Vincent, standing his ground, the SCAR roaring in his hands. Li had already started running, but when she saw him standing back there, something caught in her throat.

The scorpion zig-zagged closer, bullets sparking off its thick black carapace. Before Li could make up her mind, the creature reached Vincent, stinger rising in preparation for a strike. Then it lurched as if struck by a tank shell. Li caught the flash of green and knew at once that the scorpion had stepped on a creeper vine. Legs flailing ridiculously, the fearsome beast crumple-scrunched through a tiny hole in the ground.

"Grapple!" barked Li, grabbing John Henry and hooking him to her harness.

That was it: their lives had been endangered, and Tetris hadn't intervened. He was gone. Li spent the rest of the afternoon repeating it in her head.

"I think we can do this," said Dr. Alvarez when they turned in for the night.

"I think you're right," said Li, and punched her on the shoulder. Dr. Alvarez winced, but then a glow of pride swept over her face.

"Yeah," she said, dreamily.

"Don't get cocky, though," said Li as the scowl returned.

Two slow days later, their path ran up against a ravine. As they made their way along the edge, the undergrowth closed in, dense and tall, until they were forced into single file. Then the undergrowth turned to thornwall, a predatory plant that eviscerated anything unfortunate enough to run through it, and Li began to feel cornered.

She led the way. The ravine leered on her left, and the thornwall leaned in from the right. She felt a wetness on her cheek and sprang away, teetering on the edge. One of the plant's teeth had grazed her cheek as she passed. The skin was sliced open neatly, as if by laser beam, and her fingers came away with a vermillion sheen of blood.

A drop of something hit the ground and sizzled. Li looked up.

Eight huge spiders descended on cables of silk, spooling it dexterously from their rear ends. Another drop of venom emerged from an erect fang; she ducked out of the way as it whipped by to spit and smoke on the leaves.

"Run," she shouted, bolting for the end of the corridor, where the ravine fell away and the forest resumed, but already the calculations were completing in her mind, and she knew that the rearmost members of the group would never make it out in time—

*****

One week earlier

Tetris stalked out of the clearing, fists pulsing, and walked for ten minutes, muttering under his breath. Eventually he came to a steep slope and stopped. He leaned against a fallen branch and shook himself.

"Why am I so mad?" he cried. The anger was a radioactive orange filter over everything. He closed his eyes and rubbed them. Dagger-points of red light exploded and multiplied and faded and exploded again.

Ah, said the forest, *might be a side effect of bulking you up. Hormonal imbalance.*

"Why didn't you tell me?"

I warned you about side effects, said the forest. *But you told me to do it anyway.*

Tetris kept replaying the last blow, Vincent's eyes going unfocused as his head snapped back. Murdering him would have felt even better. Wet carnivorous pleasure. He remembered the taste of raw pillbug, the slimy salty blood. His stomach writhed. He really did want to beat the shit out of someone. The only thing that could relieve the itch in his rib cage would be to bludgeon something into twitching chunks of meat.

He looked around for something to kill, and, finding nothing, felt the bubble of anger dissipate and flow away on the breeze.

"Ah, shit," he said, and sighed. "Guess I should go apologize."

Three inattentive steps later, he stepped on a false patch of moss and plummeted into an inky abyss.

*****

Clear of the corridor, Li shouted and sprayed bullets and generally tried to distract the descending spiders from the half of the group who had yet to make it to safety. The spiders didn't notice her fire, even when it rang against their fat bellies, so focused were they on the meals at hand. Li wished for a rocket launcher, an RPG, a railgun, anything bigger than what she had, but it was no use. The lowest spider was about to reach Dr. Alvarez. Three long, evil legs crossed the void—

Something huge and sleek ripped between the trees and snatched the spider out of the air. A dragon, with leathery wings and clustered black eyes. Gouts of green blood arced as innumerable teeth snapped and popped. Then another dragon exploded out of the branches, and another. The air was thick with them, their wing-beats buffeting Dr. Alvarez and the others as they cleared the ravine and ran. Li saw three more of the spiders struck and then she was running too.

They skirted the edge of the thornwall and slid down a leafy slope, sucking air, ears bombarded by ferocious blasts of sound. The dragons swirled around them, leaping from tree to tree, but by some miracle no one was touched. At the bottom of the slope Li led them right, picking the direction at random, but then a five-story praying mantis burst full-scuttle to block their way. Its segmented razor-blade arms snapped out and descended and were promptly dismembered as three dragons tore the mantis to pieces. The head came bouncing off, a mighty compound eyeball crushed and leaking, as Li and the others cut back the way they'd come.

But the way was blocked, every path was blocked, the dragons had cordoned off all escape and were prowling along the ground, now, awkward the way a grounded eagle is awkward, tip-topping on limbs designed for flight and not stalking.

Li and the others stood in a bubble thirty feet in

diameter, around which dragons nipped and screeched and roared, and then out of the midst came the tall-striding form of Tetris, his clothes ripped, his pack gone, a smile splitting his face like a melon struck with a meat cleaver.

"Boy," said Tetris, wrapping Li in a hug that lifted her well off the ground, "have I got some shit to tell you."

12

"They don't bite," said Tetris as they walked, waving a dismissive hand in the direction of the nearest dragon. A pair of the creatures traipsed and hopped a few yards away, weaving in and out, sometimes dipping to poke a snout into a burrow or crevice, scavenging perpetually for their next meal. The ground trembled.

"If you say so," said Toni Davis. Beside her, John Henry quaked with fright, his Adam's apple bobbing.

"Where were you?" demanded Li.

"I fell down a hole," said Tetris, scratching his nose.

"I thought you had a supercomputer in your brain. How do you just fall down a hole?"

"I wasn't paying attention. Most of the past week was just lying there waiting for my bones to knit back together."

"Uh huh."

"Climbing out wasn't easy, I'll tell you that."

"What's with the dragons?"

"Apparently the forest has been working on a way to control them. Something to do with magnetism."

Tetris stopped walking, listening.

"Umm," he said, "I'm being told that the term is *electromagnetism.* Signals, encrypted and broadcast over low-band frequency—it's saying something about spectrum?"

He rolled his eyes at Li, gesticulating like someone apologizing for a over-long phone call.

"Okay, will you shut up? Nobody cares," he said to the air. "The gist of it is that the forest can send commands to dragons, but only dragons and not any other animals, because the dragons happen to have evolved some special receiver in their brains. So the forest can say, like, 'Don't eat those humans.'"

"But eat everything else."

"Well, they don't need to be told that part."

"Are we still going to the anomaly?" asked Dr. Alvarez.

"I say we put ourselves on the quickest vector out of here," said Jack Dano. It was clear that the miles were taking a toll on him.

Actually, everyone looked bad. Their once-crisp clothes hung in tatters. John Henry still wore his suit jacket under his harness. The fabric was riddled with thorn-holes and rips. All the moisture in his body seemed to leak out of his watery eyes and the pores on his cheeks. He was slick with misery, except for his lips, which were desiccated beyond recognition. But his biggest problem was that the mosquitoes loved him. He was lumpy all over with bites, red and bleeding from agitated scratching.

Later in the afternoon, a dull hum filled the air. Starting out nearly inaudible, it grew and grew until they could no longer ignore it.

"What's that noise?" asked John Henry.

Tetris turned pale, listening.

"Cut south," he said. "We'll try to go around."

"What do you mean, try?" asked Li as they crashed through the undergrowth. "Can't the dragons kill it?"

"Not this," said Tetris grimly. "We've just got to get out of its way."

They hurried on. After a while they trampled across a clearing of rotten pink flowers and came to a steep, rocky slope.

"We have to move faster," said Tetris, leading them down.

The hum had grown into an echoing drone. It was a monolithic wall of sound, and Li didn't want to think about what it meant. Nothing good, judging by the way the dragons snapped and roared.

The storm reached them a few minutes later. A swarm of tiny insects poured between the tree trunks and enveloped them. Clouds of black-bodied creatures drowned everything in a fury of buzzing wings. There were bugs of all kinds, from normal gnats and mosquitoes to beetles the size of baseball mitts. Buffeted by the storm, the dragons snapped and screeched and retired out of earshot, although every once in a while a tail could be seen whipping through the trees.

"How do we get out of this?" shouted Li into Tetris's ear.

"Just have to keep going!" he shouted back. "We're right in the middle!"

They soldiered on, squinting as hard black shells rebounded off their eyelids. Not all the insects stayed aloft. Li couldn't brush them off fast enough, and she'd learned her lesson about smashing them. The smeared blood only drew bigger bugs. A hand-sized dragonfly landed on her neck. She grasped its tumescent abdomen and flung it into the maelstrom.

John Henry screamed. A beetle had his earlobe in its pincers.

"Get it off get it off get it off!"

Vincent yanked the bug away. Most of the ear came with it. An impossible amount of blood poured out of the hole. John's shriek was lost in the roar of insects drawn by the steaming wound. He vanished under a writhing black shroud. The others crowded around, snatching and batting at the insects, but for every one they dislodged, another three zoomed to take their place. Li felt pincers biting into her skin but kept fighting, sweeping bugs away with both arms, and for a moment she managed to uncover John Henry's face—

His eyes were gone.

"Leave him!" she screamed. They plowed ahead, heads lowered, leaving John Henry a convulsing heap on the forest floor.

*****

The next morning, Tetris grapple-gunned up to a branch where Vincent, Jack Dano, and the Secret Service agent were sharing breakfast. There, as instructed by Toni Davis, he attempted to apologize. It did not go well. He was forced to retreat to Dr. Alvarez's branch to avoid a full-blown shouting match.

"Ignore them," said Dr. Alvarez.

"How do I convince them that I'm on their side?"

"It's impossible."

"People change their minds all the time."

"Hardly. Take a look at our political system."

Tetris scratched a scab on his neck. "Anybody will listen to incontrovertible proof."

"There's no such thing as incontrovertible proof," said Dr. Alvarez. She slapped a mosquito.

"Doc," said Tetris, "what's your first name?"

Dr. Alvarez gave him a long look. "Lucia."

"You wanna know mine?"

"I already do."

"Oh."

"It was all over the news."

"Right. It doesn't feel like my real name."

"I like 'Tetris.'"

"When we're back on land," he said, "do you want to get coffee?"

She laughed. "Creative."

109

"Doesn't have to be that," said Tetris. "Go-karts? Bocce ball? What do normal people do?"

"Coffee sounds great," said Dr. Alvarez.

The days passed uneventfully. Even this deep into the forest, few creatures were bold enough to challenge thirty dragons. At night their reptilian guardians filled the air with rattling snores. Gradually, the survivors grew used to their presence. Even Li's scowl began to fade. The memory of John Henry's demise kept them grounded, but with the forest on their side, it was hard to avoid feeling that survival was well within reach.

One day they came across a spiderweb that reached up to the canopy and as far as they could see in either direction. Contours of web zig-zagged from trunk to trunk.

"Can the dragons rip a hole through this?" asked Tetris.

Maybe, said the forest, *but there are six thousand spiders waiting for it to twitch.*

Tetris kicked leaves on his way back to the group. "Have to go around. Come on."

They stayed as far back as they could without losing sight of the web. The dragons, uncharacteristically wary, retreated out of earshot. It was hard to believe that the immense white wall was biological in origin. It looked like it had been there for centuries. Maybe it had. Tetris scanned the branches as he walked, but all was still.

"How are things back home?" he asked the forest.

Not great. Lots of bluster about how I'm trying to eradicate humanity.

"Wasn't that your original plan?"

Plans change.

The web went on forever. It quivered sometimes in the wind. Tree trunks, lonely columns leading into the gray distance, showed through thinner patches in the silvery wall. Hours of hiking later, there was no sign that they were getting any closer to the end.

Two dragons crashed through the undergrowth, fighting over a spike-toothed worm. The worm telescoped and writhed. When the dragons wrenched it in half, caramel goo pumped out in viscous folds.

"That's disgusting," said Davis. Beside her, Sasha Montessori looked more fascinated than alarmed. Jack Dano leaned against a tree and sighed.

"Keep going," said Tetris. "We can rest when we're on the other side."

They passed a stand of vegetation and suddenly everything fell away to their right. The ground was sandy and smooth, with no shrubs or ferns, and the trees rose like naked stakes out of the emptiness. With nothing to block his view, Tetris could see all the dragons at once, threading through the branches in the distance. They paused occasionally to preen and stretch their wings, but they never touched the ground.

The sand kills on contact, said the forest. *Keep going. It's not much further. You'll know you're close when——*

Something sucked the forest out of his head. Tetris staggered in the silence, ears ringing.

"Hey," he said. "Hello?"

No answer. The closest dragons, the ones who'd been fighting over the worm, paused mid-tussle. Their mouths hung open. Slimy eyelids slid over featureless eyeballs.

Tetris turned to face the group as the dragons lumbered into gear. "Run!"

The first dragon hurtled into their long straggly line and snapped up Sasha Montessori. One instant she was running, slim arms motoring, and the next she'd vanished down the gullet of the tumbling beast.

Li broke away from the spiderweb and led them right, toward the sand.

"Not onto the sand," shouted Tetris, but she didn't seem to hear.

The distant dragons leapt from tree to tree, closing the gap. One of them fell out of the sky, knocked down by its comrades. As soon as it touched the sand, a hundred pink tendrils exploded out, dragging it, flailing and squawking, into the depths. Li skidded and reversed direction.

Tetris heard gunfire and turned to shout at whoever it was, to tell them there was no sense in firing, but it was too late—the second dragon fell upon the Secret Service agent and shook him vigorously from side to side. The legs detached and flew.

More gunfire. Dr. Alvarez stood with her back to the spiderweb, resolutely spraying.

"No!" shouted Tetris. A third dragon swooped in. Dr. Alvarez dove aside, covering ten feet in an instant, as the dragon careened through the space where she'd been and impacted the spiderweb.

The dragon shrieked, but couldn't free itself from the viscid silk. Above, black legs whirred into motion. A host of spiders poured down the web. The dragon's struggle only enmeshed it further, but its efforts opened a hole further down the line, and it was through this hole that Dr. Alvarez led the others. Tetris, scrambling, was the last one through.

They'd just cleared the web when more dragons flung themselves against it, tangling in the sticky strands. Tetris stopped to watch as the first spiders arrived. Fueled by a fury that went beyond hunger, the spiders overran their heaving prey. Jaws snapped and crunched, popping spider abdomens like stomped-upon yogurt canisters, but there were far more arachnids than reptiles, and the scales tipped almost immediately. The dragons vanished under a churning black tide.

Tetris fled. The others had opened a considerable gap, and when he finally caught up, crashing through the undergrowth and into the clearing where they stood, he registered just a glimpse of Jack Dano raising his pistol before hurling himself down. Three bullets ripped through the air where his head had been. He scrambled in the dirt, extending a hand to say stop, but the CIA director tracked him, finger tightening.

Toni Davis pulled her own trigger. Jack Dano, struck in the arm, spun in a tight circle. The pistol pinwheeled from his hand.

"Weapons down," ordered Davis. Tetris threw his SCAR at her feet.

"What the fuck, Tetris?" said Li.

Vincent bent over Jack Dano, ripping the shirt away.

"Is he okay?" asked Tetris.

"Bandages," snapped Vincent. Dr. Alvarez slid down and removed her pack. Jack Dano's good arm lifted, the hand grasping at nothing, then fell. He hadn't made a sound.

Tetris took a quick head count. Li, Dr. Alvarez, Toni Davis, Vincent. Jack Dano, with a bullet in him. Everyone else was dead.

"He's hurt bad," said Li, examining Dano over Dr. Alvarez's shoulder.

Davis squeezed the bridge of her nose. "I'm sorry, Jack."

Dano groaned. His head lolled to the side.

"Something cut my link to the forest," said Tetris. "It must have cut the link to the dragons, too."

"If I'd known that was possible," said Li, "I never would have let them follow us."

"I didn't know either," said Tetris. "I've never lost the link before."

A cold void throbbed in the corner of his head where the forest usually lurked.

"We can stop the bleeding," said Dr. Alvarez, leaning on the wound, hands and the cloth she held both slick with blood, "but I don't know how long he's going to last."

Vincent thumbed his pistol and glared at Tetris. Toni Davis turned away, arms crossed.

"We can save him," said Tetris. "The anomaly's only a

couple days away. The forest can fix him."

"Not a fucking chance," said Vincent. "We put him on a stretcher and head for the coast."

"He won't make it," said Dr. Alvarez.

"Tetris can't even talk to the forest," said Li. "What's the point of going to the anomaly?"

"It'll come back," said Tetris.

"You don't know that."

"It's the forest, Li. It's not going anywhere."

"And yet it's gone."

"It'll come back."

She tugged her fingerless gloves tighter. "Maybe it found another conduit."

"It went away mid-sentence."

He remembered the last time he'd convinced her to go against her instincts. Had it been a mistake, in the end?

"Trust me, Li," he said.

He could tell from her eyes that she no longer did.

13

Tetris carried Jack Dano piggy-back, arms under his skinny legs, their harnesses hooked together. Every once in a while the CIA director stirred and groaned, but otherwise he laid his cheek on Tetris's shoulder and slept.

It had probably been exhaustion as much as anything that made him pull the trigger. Tetris didn't hold it against him. Not after he'd traded his pack for Jack Dano and realized the CIA director was the lighter load. Except for the C4, they'd distributed the contents of Tetris's pack across the group. The C4 was stowed in a pouch on Jack Dano's back.

They trudged silently onward, Li in front, Tetris bringing up the rear. How many weeks had it been? How many more did they have to go?

It was odd to discover that he missed the alien presence in his head.

He kept having to squash a suspicion that Dr. Alvarez would die next. She took the craziest risks. The fact that she was alive right now was an honest-to-God miracle. When he closed his eyes, her insane leap out of the dragon's path played again and again. It was only a matter of time before gambles like that caught up with her.

He'd rather somebody else took the risk next time. He really didn't want her to die. But who would he prefer in her place? Vincent? If he had to choose... Then again, since Jack Dano was already wounded, he was probably the utilitarian choice.

What if it came down to Li and Dr. Alvarez? He wanted to believe that he'd sacrifice himself to let them live.

Okay, but say that wasn't an option. Who would he choose?

Months ago, after the forest fixed him, the path forward had seemed so simple. Talk to the press, talk to the government, convince everyone to work together, save the world. How hard could it be to unite humanity when the planet faced destruction?

Pretty hard, it turned out. He was back at square one. Worse than that: he was further away from the goal than he'd been to begin with. People were dead. His appearance had splintered the world along its preexisting fault lines. For every Toni Davis, there were two or three Vincents, people who would hate and fear and distrust him no matter what he did.

Well. Maybe if he managed to avoid punching people in the face from now on, he'd have an easier time winning them over.

When they turned in for the night, Jack Dano refused his dinner-tuber and went straight to sleep. In the morning he seemed a bit more alert, and with the increased processing power came a visible surge of fear.

By the late afternoon he'd even started to talk again.

"I am going to die," he said into Tetris's ear.

"No you're not," said Tetris.

The spindly arms tightened around Tetris's neck. "Tell my wife I died saving someone. Okay?"

"You're not going to die."

"My daughters too. Lie to them. Understand?"

"Stop saying that."

Sheafs of moss hung from the lower branches, swaying lugubriously in the breeze.

"Sorry I tried to shoot you," said Jack Dano.

"It's all good."

"If this works, and I wind up like you, will you be able to read my mind?"

Tetris scrunched his nose. "I have no idea, actually."

Dano was silent for a long time.

"What's it like?" he asked at last.

"What's what like?"

"Having that thing in your head."

"It's not so bad. I miss it, actually."

"You miss it."

"It's smart. And it seems to have our best interests in mind."

"Hmph."

"Well. I guess it would be more accurate to say that its interests happen to align with ours."

Tetris had come to rely on the forest for amplified sensory data, and as a result his own senses had dulled somewhat. At his rangering prime, he would have heard the quiet rustle of air and known that a creature was diving toward him. As it was, he didn't notice anything until a shadow swept across him, and by then it was far too late.

The blood bat fell out of the sky, thirty-foot wings braking its descent. Tetris had only taken two lunging steps when the claws closed around Jack Dano and hoisted both of them off the ground. The bat launched skyward. Tetris dangled, attached by his harness, as Jack Dano released a bubbling scream. Below, Li held her fire, afraid to hit one of them. The bat shifted its grip, leaving them momentarily unmoored, then closed its claws tighter with a wet and horrible crunch. The screams ceased. Blood poured onto Tetris's neck, back and arms. He lifted his grapple gun, watching the trees whip past as he swung uncontrollably from side to side. At this speed it was almost impossible to line up a shot.

The bat approached the canopy. Tetris figured that being soaked in Jack Dano's blood increased the chances of being deemed a meal once they landed. With one hand on the latch that held the harnesses together, he aimed the grapple gun and waited. There would only be one chance. If he missed, he'd free fall two hundred feet, which would turn him into a green pancake not even the forest could fix.

He took a deep breath, squinted, detached himself, and fired.

For a moment he floated. Then the hook caught a branch. He slammed the button; the line yanked him forward as he began to reel it in. The speed of the swing was uncontrollable. Rising, he careened toward an inconveniently-located tree—

He raised an arm to protect his face and bounced hard off the bark. The skin on his arms and legs tore open, but his bones seemed more or less intact. Rebounding, he ascended to the branch where his line was wrapped.

The blood bat screeched. Tetris peered into the canopy and caught a flash of wing. He'd jumped off just short of its nest. Blood welled from his scrapes. He remembered the C4 on Jack Dano's back and grimaced. It didn't make sense to leave it. He'd sneak into the nest, grab the pack, and find his way back to the others.

It couldn't be more than an hour until dark. He'd have to move quickly. Luckily, the bat hadn't carried him far, and he was pretty sure he knew which direction to go. He'd trust Li and the others to wait for him.

When he crested the edge of the nest, it was already deserted. Jack Dano's husk lay in the corner, the clothes tattered, two red craters in the chest where the fangs had entered. Tetris tried not to look at the face.

As he retrieved the pack, a torrent of psychic energy flooded his skull. He fell against the wall and vomited. His vision whirled. His stomach did backflips. It felt like somebody had shunted six thousand volts directly into his spinal column. He fell to his knees, clutching his head. The nausea and headache and swirling dizziness intensified until, right when he thought he was going to pass out, the assault relented.

Sorry about that, said the forest.

"Where did you go?"

No time. Get the pack and move.

*****

Li walked in tight circles, kicking the weeds.

"He's not coming back," said Vincent.

"He'll come back," said Li.

"We've had this discussion."

"I was right last time."

"He's bat food."

"Dano's bat food. Tetris just happened to be attached."

"How will he locate us?" asked Dr. Alvarez.

"He'll find us," said Toni Davis. "We're staying put."

It always amazed Li that everyone listened to Davis the first time she said something.

"Davis," said Li.

"Yeah?"

"I thought about your offer."

"And?"

The ground swelled, cakes of dirt crumbling to reveal an expanse of orange-brown exoskeleton. A giant crab, awakened from its slumber, shuddered to the surface. Li and the others scattered, firing into spiky corners of shell as the beast rose on segmented legs. Li's bullets sent an eyeball bouncing back on its stalk. The crab skittered left. Toni Davis tried to dive out of the way, but she was too slow, and one of the sharp feet pinned her thigh to the ground.

Davis didn't make a sound, just rolled away when the crab passed, clutching the wound. The crab must have smelled the blood, because after a few steps it wheeled and faced her, weathering the fusillade with one claw clacking greedily. Li fired and shouted and ran closer, but the crab only had eyes for Davis.

Then a blood-drenched Tetris came hurtling out of the trees, free-falling the final fifteen feet as his grappling hook whistled down behind him. He landed on the crab's back like a spider and slapped something against it. The crab bucked and grasped, flinging Tetris away. He slammed against a tree trunk and pressed the detonator.

A yellow-orange globe of flame bloomed on the crab's back. Li ducked as a shell-shard the size of a manhole cover whizzed past. Razor-edged fragments embedded in tree trunks like ninja stars. Then a rain of half-seared crab meat filled the clearing with a salty crustacean reek. Li's ears rang, but she rushed to Davis's side, hefting the Secretary of State up and over her shoulder. Four grapple guns popped, and they zipped into the safety of the branches as the cries of creatures drawn by the explosion began to rend the air.

Li worked to contain the bleeding, her hands crimson and slick. Davis had passed out. Her mouth hung open, and her head tilted lightly as they shifted her. Everything they wrapped around the ruined leg soaked through in moments.

"We're close to the anomaly," said Tetris. "We can get

there before dark."

"That's only forty-five minutes," said Li. Below them, centipedes fought over a crab leg. A maggoty creature slurped its sucker-mouth across gently smoking shell.

"She's not going to last through the night," said Tetris. "She's not going to last two hours, Li. We're really close. We don't have to get all the way there. Just close enough."

"I take it the forest's back?" said Dr. Alvarez.

"Yeah."

"Where'd it go?"

Tetris hefted Toni Davis and hooked her to his harness. Vincent held his head in his hands. Li watched him carefully. With Davis unconscious, he might become a threat, but that was a problem for later.

"North Korea launched a nuke at a nerve center in the Pacific," said Tetris. "Took down the whole global system. Caused a reboot, basically, the way it's being described to me."

They swung away from the chaos and descended when the coast was clear. Tetris sprinted ahead with Toni Davis cradled in his arms. Li and the others pounded after him.

When they reached a ravine, Tetris wasted no time securing his line around a tree trunk.

"Is she going to be alright?" asked Dr. Alvarez.

Davis's slack-mouthed face shone in the dusk.

"It has to do to her what it did to me," said Tetris, "so I really have no idea."

He stepped over the edge and rappelled into darkness.

That night, Li dreamed she was in Toni Davis's White

House office. The Secretary of State was nowhere to be found. Li sat in the leather chair and drank in the aroma of books and ancient furniture. After a while she noticed that she still wore her clothes from the forest and stood with a start. She'd gotten mud all over the room. She planned on sneaking out before someone noticed the mess, but when she flung the door open there was nothing on the other side but the plunging red gullet of a subway snake.

In the morning, as she waited with Dr. Alvarez and Vincent at the edge of the ravine, it occurred to Li that two universes were about to diverge. In one, Toni Davis would survive. She'd emerge, transformed, from the pit. They would make it to shore, find the nearest US Embassy, and from there Li and Tetris would have only a small part to play. Davis would retake her position as Secretary of State. She would win over the world's leaders and unify all of humanity. Then, together with the forest, they would fend off the alien invasion.

In the second universe, Toni Davis would die. But no matter how hard she tried, Li couldn't figure out what happened after that. The second future was a bleak wall of fog. Her mind hit it and glanced off.

So Li focused on the universe she could comprehend. She imagined talking to the press, discussing their journey, making the argument that Davis should be appointed Secretary again despite her green skin. She imagined working for Davis in her office, Davis practicing her speeches, her calls for humanity to confront the threat together.

When Tetris's head poked over the lip of the ravine, Li was still running through plans for the future, weighing the most politically correct response to this or that journalistic inquiry, foiling hypothetical attempts on the Secretary's life, when it dawned on her that Tetris was alone, and his arms were empty, and the universe she'd landed in was, impossibly, the second one, the one too awful to imagine.

14

Someone in the back of Zip's head kept saying in a small and garbled voice that it was time to consider maybe getting out of the shower, where he'd been for an indeterminate but undoubtedly prodigious number of minutes, and put on his clothes to go meet Hollywood in the lobby. Unless he wanted to be late. He didn't particularly want to be late, but then he didn't particularly want to get out of the shower, either. It was extremely warm in here. The hotel room was colder than the polar wastes by comparison.

He stood on his one magnificent leg, the prominent muscles of which flexed and twitched incessantly, thousands of microscopic readjustments together producing the kind of balance that two-legged people assumed without thinking. Every once in a while he touched the wall to correct himself when he tilted too far, but never more than a light brush of his fingers. Never once a lean.

Well. When he needed to turn around, for instance to turn up the heat, he had no choice but to lean. Or hold onto something and hop and twist. He did this now, hopping and twisting, wishing for the steel bar he'd installed in his shower back home, when suddenly the frictionless floor let him go.

His first instinct was to reach with the phantom leg to arrest his descent. Instead all he found was a faceful of shower curtain, followed by more shower curtain (it felt for a moment as though he were thrashing through a bottomless pit of shower curtains), followed by the cold ceramic edge of the toilet bowl.

Rolling on the fake tile, he ripped the curtain away. Water ramping off the fabric and his glistening body created a lake on the bathroom floor. He planted a hand on the toilet seat and levered himself up, then lunged into the tub and turned off the water.

The mirror revealed a bruise on his cheek already beginning to blossom. Zip toweled off and went to get dressed.

"What happened to your face?" asked Hollywood downstairs, with a grin that said he knew the answer.

Zip ignored him and tore into the free continental breakfast.

"I seem to recall you saying you didn't need a handicapped room," said Hollywood.

"Blow me," said Zip around a mouthful of croissant.

Across the room, a woman wearing nothing but yellow—yellow sundress, yellow shoes, a pair of yellow-rimmed sunglasses perched in her shiny black hair—read the newspaper while she pushed oatmeal around in a disposable bowl. The curves of her face converged on a pair of lips held in prim repose. Her chin jutted defiantly. Zip felt a pang of inscrutable sadness.

"In global news," said the television suspended behind Hollywood, "tensions in East Asia remain high following North Korea's launch of a nuclear missile into the Pacific Forest."

The spot where the prosthetic connected to Zip's leg stump was itching again. He undid the straps, letting the leg hang loose, and vigorously scratched the area beneath.

"Japanese leaders are calling for renewed sanctions on North Korea, citing the nuclear missile's path over mainland Japan as a violation of international law, but the effectiveness of any sanctions will depend on China's agreement and participation. As of this morning, Beijing still has yet to comment on the matter. It remains unclear whether the strike was carried out in cooperation with, or against the wishes of, North Korea's largest ally."

"This is exactly the kind of shit that's going to make us rich," said Hollywood, pointing at the TV.

"I fail to see how the first deployment of a nuclear weapon in eighty years could possibly be viewed as a positive."

"Well, it shows you that people are losing their minds. And since our whole business model depends on swindling crazy rich people, I'd say the future looks lucrative."

"Money won't mean anything once the apocalypse hits."

"That's exactly what our customers think. Hell, I think we should triple our rates."

The yellow-clad girl's left arm was sleeved in a complicated tattoo. Zip thought he could make out a spider entwined in the design, its long legs arcing around her bicep.

"We haven't even run our first expedition yet," he said. "What if everybody dies? Who's going to be dumb enough to sign up the second time?"

The grin spread across Hollywood's face like a rash. "Two words: security deposits. I've got expeditions booked out for months. Any time somebody gets cold feet, I—we—pocket two hundred grand."

Zip whistled. The girl turned at the sound and stared him down. After a moment he had to look away. When he glanced back she was perusing the newspaper again.

"Our rates are a joke," he said.

"Why do you think I'm always laughing?"

They'd rented a campground outside Seattle for the training. Hollywood drove Zip out in a pickup truck laden with supplies. On the main field, ten minutes before the trainees were scheduled to arrive, Zip jogged a few laps, testing out the prosthetic.

Hollywood slipped a flask into his jacket as Zip lurched to a halt in front of him.

"You mind if I get out of here?" said Hollywood, "I have business things to attend to."

"Business things."

"Interviews," said Hollywood. "We've gotta get multiple expeditions running at once, right? Which means we need more guides."

"As long as my cut doesn't change."

"Jeez, dude, we signed papers, didn't we? In the business world, paper is sacred."

"Uh huh."

"These guys will get a sliver of my share. I've got it all figured out. Don't worry about that. You're looking at a born entrepreneur, here."

"Douglas Douglas, CEO."

"Zachary Chase, Executive Vice President of Customer Ballbreaking."

"Does have a nice ring to it."

"Make these fuckers cry, Zip. It's for their own good."

As Hollywood pulled away, a dilapidated bus carrying the trainees came trundling around the edge of the trees. The distant peak of Mt. Rainier stared down disapprovingly. Zip waited beside the supply crates, savoring the full-bodied aroma of pine trees and earth.

The trainees spilled out of the bus talking and laughing like twelve-year-olds arriving at summer camp. Half of them wore flip-flops. Zip spotted a couple of dresses among the female recruits.

"Your clothes," he moaned.

No one heard him. The bus driver had popped open the luggage areas on the sides of the bus, and the recruits were busy sorting through their gear. One woman let out a laugh so piercing that Zip couldn't help but wince.

"Shut up," he shouted.

Thirty wide eyes swiveled to face him.

"What are you wearing?" he demanded. "How are you going to run in flip-flops?"

Nobody answered, so he focused his glare on one woman in particular.

"Run?" she said. "Today's the first day. I didn't think we'd—"

"Yeah," cut in one of the chubbier men. "Orientation, right? There's never—I mean, it's the first day."

Zip massaged his jaw. Their clothes were spotless and visibly expensive, as were their gear bags and tents. The confidence with which they held their pale millionaire bodies made him want to grab and shake them one by one. Made him want to pummel them until they sniveled and groveled at his feet.

"Drop the bags," said Zip.

"I thought you wanted us to change shoes?"

He stared at her, fighting the red film settling over his vision.

"If it's running you intend us to do," said a man in his fifties, "you might could allow us to don appropriate attire beforehand."

"Fine," said Zip. "You have three minutes to change."

"Where?" cried a woman in a floral dress.

"Three minutes!"

He walked away, counting the seconds under his breath. These people would never respect him the way he'd respected Rivers. They were too entitled, too used to getting exactly what they wanted. He'd make them miserable. Break them down. Tear their egos to shreds and stuff the shreds down their mottled, fleshy throats.

"Six laps," said Zip when the group had reassembled. "The bottom five do a seventh lap while the rest of you rest."

The trainees gaped.

"Well?" he said, pointing at the edge of the field.

"What," said one woman, "you mean, like, now?"

"Yes. Now."

One by one, they began to jog.

"Faster," shouted Zip.

It was like watching a herd of well-fed antelope wobbling toward a watering hole. Zip turned away, stomach wriggling with rage. He wasn't sure why he was so mad. Maybe it was all these perfectly functional legs attached to such pampered, wasted bodies.

"I don't envy you a bit," said the bus driver, and whistled.

Zip kept them moving all afternoon. When they weren't running, they were alternating push-ups and sit-ups, or hiking along the trails that encircled the campground. When the sun began to dip beneath the treeline, the trainees were considerably quieter than they'd been that morning, and had acquired a satisfactory coat of filth. Zip rounded them up near their luggage for a final word as Hollywood's pickup came rumbling around the corner.

"Congratulations," he said, "you're all hopeless."

The general response to this statement was a groan.

"I mean that seriously. None of you are qualified for this. Odds are pretty good that you're going to die. But if you work hard—if you work hard, and you listen to me—I may be able to improve your chances. A little."

The pickup truck rolled to a stop. Moths danced in the headlight beams.

"You're not sleeping here?" warbled one of the trainees, empty tent bag drooping from his hand.

"What a hilarious question," said Zip as he hauled himself into the truck.

"What about bears?" asked another recruit.

Hollywood leaned across Zip and beamed.

"Ladies and gentlemen," he said, "if you're afraid of bears, the forest will make you shit your pants."

Zip slammed the door as they rolled away.

"How'd it go?" asked Hollywood.

"They're hopelessly out of shape and grossly incompetent, I hate them, and I'm pretty sure they hate me too."

"Excellent," said Hollywood. "How much progress do you think you can make in a month?"

"Absolutely none," said Zip.

"Well," said Hollywood as they rattled over a gulch, "as long as they end up thinking they made progress, I suppose that's all that matters."

Zip stared out the window into the shifting green darkness.

Back at the hotel, he went looking for the girl in yellow, but the bar was deserted. He didn't see a single human being on the way to his room. The hotel was quiet as a morgue, although a slight hum filled its halls. A gash of plywood peeked through his door above the card slot. He had to swipe five times before it let him in. Inside he stripped to his boxers, flung everything in a pile, and fell into bed.

Five minutes later, somebody knocked on the door.

"No thank you," said Zip, and rolled over, pulling the blankets tighter.

The knocks came again, twice as forceful as before.

"Go away," shouted Zip. Probably a drunk who'd picked the wrong room.

The knocks kept coming.

Zip yanked the cord to turn on the light and leapt out of bed. He hopped across the room, not bothering with the prosthetic, and tugged the door open. In the hall stood a small man with a ferocious nose.

"Hello," said the man.

"What do you want?"

"My name is George," said the man.

"Thanks for sharing. What do you *want*?"

"I would like to join your next expedition."

Zip scratched the back of his head.

"Talk to my boss," he said.

"I did," said the man. "But he wasn't interested."

Zip snorted. "If you had the money, I don't see why he'd turn you down."

"That's the thing."

"Well, then, buddy, you're out of luck. We're not a charity. We are, in fact, the polar opposite of a charity."

"Please."

"Look, you're actually the lucky one, okay? All these other people—they're fucked. You realize that, right? They're almost certainly going to die. This whole thing is a scam. We just figured we'd try to get some money out of them before they went out there on their own."

"I know it's dangerous."

"Jeez, man, the answer is no. I'm sorry."

The man's eyes watered. He wiped them curtly on his sleeve.

"Did you know my son?" he asked.

Zip leaned his head against the doorframe. "Who?"

"Because you were a ranger, I mean. I think they called him Tetris?"

Zip stared.

"He was the one—you know, the green one. The one in the news."

"Holy shit," said Zip. "You're Tetris's dad?"

"You knew him?"

"Now I definitely can't let you go."

"No!"

"Jesus, man, just because he might be dead doesn't mean you have to follow him down."

There were real tears in the man's eyes. He kept swiping at them, but it only smeared the moisture across his face.

"I just want to say goodbye," he said.

Zip considered that for a moment. "How's going into the forest supposed to help?"

Somewhere down the hall, an ice machine gargled.

"If part of the forest wound up in him," said Tetris's dad, "don't you think it's possible that part of him wound up in it?"

15

"Him again?" said Hollywood when he arrived at the hotel and found Zip and George sharing breakfast.

"Hear me out," said Zip.

The smile rotted and fell away. "Absolutely not."

"It's Tetris's dad."

"I don't care if he's the Pope. No money, no trip. It's that simple."

Zip pushed a hand through his hair. "I knew this would happen."

Hollywood squinted but didn't say anything.

"Take his ticket out of my share," said Zip.

"Ha!"

"I'm serious."

"You want to pay two million dollars to probably get your best friend's grieving father killed? Shit, Zip, if you want him dead that bad, I know people who'll handle it for four hundred bucks."

"Just promise you'll keep him alive."

"I'm going to try to keep them all alive, *Zachary*. That doesn't mean it's going to happen."

"Sit down," Zip said to George. George remained standing.

The scrambled eggs had lost whatever watery flavor they'd had to begin with. The breakfast rolls tasted like ash. Zip pushed his plate back. The girl in the yellow sundress was nowhere to be found. She'd probably checked out. Somehow the fact that he'd never see her again seemed like the real tragedy in all of this.

When they pulled up to the training camp, Zip almost laughed at the tents, which were clumped so close together that the trainees were having trouble extricating themselves.

"Who's he?" demanded someone, pointing an indignant finger at George.

"He showed up late," said Zip.

"Where's his tent?"

George's possessions were limited to a ratty backpack and a green sleeping bag.

"Somebody gets to share," said Zip.

Groans.

"Whoever lets my good friend George sleep in their tent can skip the first two laps," said Zip.

Nobody volunteered, although a few trainees winced, stretching creaking muscles.

"Let's try that again. In five seconds, you're all running laps until somebody volunteers."

A man with thick eyebrows proffered a pudgy hand. Zip clapped once, a gunshot-sound. Several trainees jumped.

"Magnificent. Show him the way."

George tiptoed through the maze of stakes and tent-lines after the bushy-eyebrowed man. The others grumbled. Zip felt a speech coming on.

"Sixty million generations ago," he said, "your ancestors were snot-nosed rats sniveling in tunnels carved from dinosaur shit. Those ancestors relied on fear to survive. Nothing has changed. I can fill your brain with knowledge, but the most important trait to foster is cowardice. In the forest, you are prey. You are a cocktail sausage. A couple of you," he paused, scratching his nose, "are sticks of beef jerky, or hemispheres of ham. But all of you are food. Is that clear?"

He could tell that they wanted to roll their eyes, but were prevented from doing so by the desire to avoid additional laps.

Well. He'd never paid attention to the speeches Rivers gave, either. Although then, at least, he'd had the excuse of being a teenager.

*****

The man who'd agreed to let George sleep in his tent was coincidentally also named George, although everyone

141

called him by his last name, which was Matherson. He owned a chain of dealerships that sold tractors, forklifts, cherry-pickers, and other equipment of similar scale. His net worth was around fourteen million dollars; he was spending two million on this expedition.

Sherry would never would have allowed it.

He was alone in a fast-decaying world. People were loud and selfish, and more and more of them were adopting ideas he found repulsive. He quarantined those trends in the corner of his brain labeled "Concerning But Ultimately Not Worth Worrying About." Though it gave him great satisfaction, during election season, to stamp a big red "NO" on all the depravity. Still, at the end of the day, it didn't bother him. It didn't. People were going to do whatever they were going to do. He just wished they would stop shoving his face in it.

The worrying thing was that his side kept losing, and sooner or later he figured he was going to have to choose between presidential candidates who BOTH thought it was okay for men to marry each other, and women to recklessly murder their babies, and when that happened it would probably sicken him so much that he'd retreat from politics entirely, and cancel his cable subscription, and live out the rest of his days on the porch of his ranch house, watching the wind ruffle the trees and nursing an American beer while his Mexican gardener (the legal kind) drove neat loops around the enormous lawn in a high-end mower taken directly from the stock of Matherson Mid-sized Machinery.

At least that had been the plan until the forest business took off. Matherson had seen the Green Ranger on television and known at once that he was staring at the next step in human evolution. Online he found hundreds of forums obsessing over the forest and the Green Ranger himself. "Immortality" was the word being bandied about. Rumormongers said that the forest could mend wounds, cure illnesses, and bestow eternal youth. Some even claimed that the transformation allowed you to read minds. The nuttiest of the nutty went so far as to suggest that the transformation enabled photosynthesis, so that you'd never have to eat again.

He'd tried to squelch the idea. Opened two new dealerships, commissioned television ads, stayed up late crunching numbers... but there was only so much to do. He always had time left over. He took a month-long vacation, sat around Italian cafes trying to look comfortable, and snapped pictures of the idiotic tourists pretending to prop up the Leaning Tower of Pisa. The trip only stressed him out more.

He even gave online dating a try, but every woman who expressed interest was chubby, ugly, or both. This infuriated him. He had money, right? Where were all the gold diggers?

The longer it continued, the more the purposeless thumb-twiddling life began to grate on him, and the larger the Green Ranger loomed in his imagination. He read dozens of books about the forest, binge-watched old ranger programs, and hired a personal trainer. Thirty pounds slipped off him in four months, leaving him a spry two hundred and twenty, practically an Olympic long-jumper, or so he quite humorously remarked to his employees.

Once the idea took root, it was impossible to think about anything else. So when Matherson heard about Hollywood's program—run by real rangers!—all the self-control came crumbling down at once.

*****

"Man, I'd give three branches—bank branches—for a decent rib eye," said Bob Bradley, prodding the Vienna sausages that wallowed in yellow preservative goo on his damp paper plate.

The others ate in silence, watching the campfire kick up sparks. George Aphelion, forty-nine years old, matted clumps of hair protruding from the edges of his sweat-streaked bald spot, shins borderline splinted, nose jutting huge and defiant as ever—father with a grand total of zero extant children, down from a peak of two—sniffed one of his own Vienna sausages, steeled himself, and wolfed it down whole. The processed meat cylinder hit his stomach with gruesome force. He gulped water from a canteen.

"Yes, three branches," said Bob Bradley, examining a sausage's pallid casing. "Three branches. I think I could spare those."

He peered around the somnolent circle and decided to make it absolutely clear:

"I've got seventeen, you know, so I really think I could spare three without much trouble. For a good well-done steak."

Rosalina, she of the withering laugh: "Branches?"

"Bank branches," repeated Bob Bradley, beaming.

"How cute," said Rosalina. "Do you give out credit cards with little panda bears on them?"

The smile curdled. "No."

"Now, my husband," said Rosalina, shoulder-patting her husband, whose name nobody knew—he was "Rosalina's husband" to them, which seemed to suit him fine—"my husband owns a law practice. How many law offices do we have, again, honey?"

Rosalina's husband grunted.

"That was it. Fifteen! So—not quite as many."

"No, not quite as many," said Bob, putting his plate down and crossing his meaty arms.

"Of course, it's not a one-to-one comparison. A good law office... well, I don't have to tell you how much money a good law firm pulls in. You're an economically-inclined individual, Bob, ah ha ha ha!"

George Aphelion cleared his plate. He breathed deeply, trying to calm his wriggling stomach.

"Although I don't think my husband would trade even one of those law offices for something as ephemeral as a steak. He built them from nothing, you understand. Pulled himself up the mountain by his bootstraps. Those offices mean an awful heaping lot to him!"

"I built my business from scratch as well," said Bob in

a not-quite whine. "I wouldn't actually trade—that's ridiculous."

"Banks," said Rosalina. "What a nice business. Fun! You have those little pipes, right? The ones that shoot capsules back and forth?"

"Of course we have those," said Bob, stabbing a sausage so hard that two tines of his plastic fork went careening into the darkness. "Those are an integral element of the modern banking business model. We'd be fools not to leverage such technology."

"How fun," said Rosalina.

Across the campfire, George Matherson, of Matherson Mid-sized Machinery, chewed and swallowed and chewed and swallowed. He'd learned early on that his own fortunes were pitiable compared to those of the more-successful trainees. When the others asked him what he did, he told them curtly that he ran his own business, and left it at that.

"Well," said Rosalina, "We've finally learned what everyone does for a living."

The fire crackled and spat.

"Except you," said Rosalina, pointing a long finger at George Aphelion, who froze with a pilfered sausage (Bob's) halfway to his mouth.

"Um," said George.

"What did you say your name was, again?"

"George," said George.

"What do you do for a living, George?"

He placed his fork down. "I'm a toll booth operator."

Open mouths coruscated in the firelight.

"I don't like it very much," he offered.

"Well," said Rosalina, affixing a smile to her plasticized face, "I suppose you meet a lot of awful interesting people. That must be nice!"

Rosalina's husband made a noise like a constipated hippopotamus.

"Not really," said George. "You don't really get to meet anyone, to be honest. They drive right by."

The corners of Rosalina's eyes scrunched up. "Well, no, I'm sure they just, hmm. But how good of you, though, looking out for the common man? Somebody has to do it, after all. Somebody must. Maintain the integrity of our highways, and so on."

"How are you paying for this?" blurted Bob Bradley.

"Bob!" said Rosalina, hand fluttering before her throat.

"I'm not," said George, and flung a fistful of pine needles into the fire.

"That's not fair," said Matherson. The others sounded their agreement. "I've got half a mind to demand a refund."

"The instructor's paying my share," said George.

The murmurs intensified.

"Playing favorites," said Bob. "I should have known. That slimy, one-legged little-"

"Hey," said George.

Bob shut his mouth.

"Easy, boys," said Rosalina. "I'm sure there was a good reason for Mr. Chase's largesse."

She eyed George, hoping he'd share, but the toll booth operator only stared into the fire.

16

After they completed their training, the would-be-adventurers were allowed two weeks to recuperate. They exchanged handshakes and back slaps in the parking lot before climbing into turbocharged European sports coupes and roaring away. George Aphelion sat on the curb tossing a pebble in the air.

"Go home, George," said Zip.

"Home has been repossessed," said George. The pebble flew, hung at its apex, and plummeted back to his hand.

"Whatever," said Hollywood, and turned to go.

Zip sat on the curb beside George and watched two ants try to drag a dead beetle out of a crack in the asphalt.

"You think we're ready to go in there?" asked George.

Zip said nothing. The ants had the beetle on the edge

of the crevice. They tugged and tugged. One of them lost its grip, and the payload tumbled to its original position. The ants climbed down and resumed their efforts.

"I'll take that as a no," said George.

"Hungry?" asked Zip.

George nodded.

"Come on," said Zip, and levered himself to his feet.

They went to Thai Restaurant and sat on the patio. It was the kind of cloudy day that looked like it should have been colder than it was. George flipped through the menu, frown lines engaged.

"Do they have a hamburger?"

Zip laughed. "Please."

"I don't like ethnic food," said George.

"How Midwestern of you."

George's mouth twitched.

"Look," said Zip, "just get pad Thai. White people love pad Thai."

George found it in the menu. "Not a fan of shrimp."

"Get it with chicken. You'll like it. It's like sweet and spicy pasta."

The waitress filled their glasses with clinking ice water.

"We used to go here all the time," said Zip.

George played with the paper tube from his straw, wrapping it around his index finger.

"Tetris didn't like 'ethnic food' either. I always blamed it on y'all."

George didn't respond.

"I'm just kidding, man, sorry," said Zip.

"I wasn't a very good father," said George.

Zip blew air through pursed lips. "And here we were, having such a normal conversation, too."

A group of sparrows hopped and twittered on an empty table. Every once in a while, a gust of wind sent them fluttering, but they always returned, rearranging their positions, little heads rotating inquisitively.

"Being a parent is hard?" said Zip. "Is that what you want me to say?"

George crushed his straw-paper spiral into a ball.

"I can't shake the feeling that Tetris isn't dead," said Zip.

"Don't taunt me."

"He and Li chased me down a chasm and carried me two weeks out of the forest. A plane crash is nothing."

George examined his chopsticks. Tried to hold them, failed, and set them next to his plate.

"I see a little bit of that in you," said Zip. "The stubbornness, I mean."

"Will stubbornness help me survive?"

"Absolutely not. Have you listened to anything I've said?"

"The louder bits."

"Look," said Zip, "here's the most important lesson. You ready?"

George nodded.

"If you ever have the chance to risk your life to save someone else," said Zip, "let them die."

George twisted his nose histrionically when he tasted

his pad Thai. Then he cleared his plate, scraping up every last bit of noodle and sauce, and chewed mournfully on a toothpick until Zip ordered him a second serving.

*****

Counting George Aphelion, there were sixteen men and women in the first batch of explorers. Eight of them went into the forest with Hollywood; the other eight went with a bearlike ranger named Bo Jr.

Both Georges were in Hollywood's group, along with Bob Bradley, Rosalina Waters, and her husband. There was a young British millionaire named Jeremy Mitchell, who never stopped smiling, and a burly man named Roger Murlock, who communicated largely in grunts, and therefore got along swimmingly with Rosalina's husband. They'd often been seen sharing a cigar during boot camp evenings, sitting a comfortable distance away from one another on a thick log. The final member of the group was a man named Frank, whose laserlike attention to Zip's words during training betrayed a military background. Frank was not fucking around. He was the first trainee to master the grapple gun, and the only one who displayed any proficiency whatsoever with a firearm (everyone had been issued a 10mm handgun as something of a formality).

It was illegal for civilians to enter the forest from the American coastline, so Hollywood drove them across the

Mexican border in a dilapidated bus. Bo Jr. followed in a truck laden with supplies, his windows down, strands of reggae blasting out and sometimes wafting through the rear windows of the bus.

"Why didn't you hire a driver?" asked Bob Bradley, appalled to see his expedition's leader driving a bus like a common laborer.

"I've got my margin to think of," said Hollywood.

This earned begrudging nods from the self-made businessmen among them.

"Can we stop by the outlets in San Ysidro?" asked Rosalina. "My mother used to take me there on weekends."

"Nope," said Hollywood, and thumbed a CD out of a black plastic carrying case. "Everyone sit down and shut up."

The rest of the drive, he bombarded them with Outkast, the Jurassic Five, and A Tribe Called Quest. The only explorer who nodded along, even mouthing a few of the words to "Hey Ya," was Roger Murlock, earning him a wounded glare from Rosalina's husband.

South of Tijuana, Hollywood pulled off onto a dirt road and rumbled toward the coast. The Mexican coastline was dotted with tiny huts, each with a single satellite dish. Hollywood parked beside one of these outposts and jumped out, speaking in rapid but broken Spanish to the Mexican Coast Guard representative who came out to meet him. After everyone had trickled out, the guardsman leapt into the driver's seat and drove the bus away.

"He stole your bus!" said George Matherson.

"It's his bus, Einstein," said Hollywood.

Matherson seemed unconvinced.

As George Aphelion stood before the towering treeline, ancient memories barraged him, childhood trips with his parents into the Blue Ridge Mountains, camping in Shenandoah National Park... streams and waterfalls and trees that had seemed as titanic at the time as the ones in front of him now.

Looking into the forest was like staring down the green-black gullet of infinity. So why wasn't he afraid?

He breathed deeply as they hiked. The ground sloped gently beneath his feet. Thick, earthy air expanded long-withered regions of his lungs. Birds and insects whizzed and sang all around them, and squirrels caroused in the undergrowth. A goofy grin crept across George's face. The forest felt like home.

Nothing happened the first two days. Hollywood led the way, chewing bubble gum, pointing out traps for them to avoid. The first creeper vine appeared halfway through their second day; the first spider trapdoor, just before their second evening.

On the third day, they came across a stand of stunning turquoise flowers.

"Don't touch those," said Hollywood as he passed.

Jeremy Mitchell, the wily British millionaire, winked at the others and bent his head to take a great whiff.

"Simply marvelous," he whispered, knobby fingers brushing the petals.

The next morning, a wild boar the size of a post office came rumbling around a stand of razorgrass.

"Grapple guns!" barked Hollywood, aiming and firing in a single smooth motion.

Blood thu-thunked in George's head. Like the others, he'd fired a grapple gun hundreds of times in training, but the mountain of pigflesh growing in his peripheral vision had erased all confidence. He aimed, bit his tongue, and fired.

The hook crossed the vertical space in slow motion. It paused at its apex and descended, wrapping around the branch.

George slammed the button, bracing himself, and welcomed the tug against his harness as the grapple gun rocketed him skyward. Safe high above, he conducted a quick census. Eight, counting Hollywood and himself. Where was the ninth?

Gunshots popped. Far below, Frank, who'd shown so much promise in training, stood suicidally firm, grapple gun untouched, firing his pistol two-handed, the gun kicking up with each shot. He pumped a full magazine into the charging boar. Then, as he reloaded—stupendously calm, hands moving deftly, no hint of fear—it hit him.

The tusks weren't even necessary. The boar's snout knocked him down and under the hooves as the beast tried and failed to slurp him up on the first pass. By the time it wheeled around, Frank was bloody trampled meat, which the boar promptly tossed down its throat.

"Fucking idiot," said Hollywood.

The boar stared blearily up at them. It snorted. Pawed the ground. Nudged their tree with its snout. Then, after one last baleful glare, it departed, gargantuan hindquarters rolling, brown fur bristling over prodigious slabs of muscle.

"Stupid motherfucker," said Hollywood, wiping his pale-green face. "You stupid, stupid motherfucker."

17

Jeremy Mitchell soon stopped smiling. He staggered along, eyes glazed, until Hollywood asked him what the matter was. The British millionaire prepared to speak, and an army of tiny black beetles came swarming out of his open mouth.

"You touched them!" yelped Hollywood, leaping back as Jeremy convulsed to the ground. "You fucking Neanderthal! I told you not to!"

As Jeremy gurgled and wriggled, his skin erupted from head to toe, innumerable beetles fighting their way free. Hollywood raised his SCAR several times, but didn't pull the trigger, though it clearly pained him. As the others

157

backed away, scratching arms and scalps that suddenly itched furiously, Hollywood knelt a safe distance from Jeremy and bowed his head.

"I tried to warn you," he said.

Roger Murlock stepped up and put a bullet through Jeremy's skull. Two mornings later, when a flesh wasp snatched Murlock, stung him, and dropped him in a gully, a larva wriggling in the depths of his paralyzed gut, Hollywood returned the favor.

On the sixth day, a pack of squawking velociraptors hurtled down a slope to their right, feathers rustling. Sickle claws flashed. Three feet high, the reptiles would have posed relatively little threat if they hadn't come in such astounding numbers. Hollywood sprayed down several as they descended, then drew an enormous hunting knife and launched into the fray. The silver blade flashed from target to target like a bolt of steely lightning. The ferocity of his attack, combined with frenzied pistol fire from the other explorers, quickly routed the raptors, sending them screeching into the jungle, but not before Rosalina's husband had his throat ripped out.

Bob Bradley missed a grapple and was torn in half by a pair of scorpions.

Rosalina tripped on a leaf-scattered slope and tumbled down, landing against a funnel-shaped silvery web. George Aphelion, standing at the top of the hill, battled an urge to follow. Before he could decide, a green-bodied spider came around the edge of the web, and the question of whether to risk his life was rendered wholly moot.

George Matherson dreamed of his dead wife. She stood in a undulating field of tall grass and smiled wider than he'd ever seen her smile. The sun beamed down and set her hair ablaze. He went to her, crying, but just as he reached his arms out to embrace her, he woke to the same dusky forest. Two hours later, he stepped on a creeper vine and vanished forever into the abyss.

Just like that, Hollywood and George Aphelion were alone.

*****

"I really thought I could do it," said Hollywood, legs dangling off the branch.

George Aphelion examined a gigantic bug bite on his arm. "Keep them alive, you mean."

Hollywood spat off the edge.

"You thought you could keep them alive," said George.

"No. God, no."

"Then what?"

"How did they get so rich if they were stupid, huh? Answer me that."

George scraped the bug bite with a couple of fingernails. Dark blood oozed out. He didn't feel anything at all.

"It's like when you make up your mind to dump a girl," said Hollywood, tugging at a loose edge of bark. "You get all the reasons straight in your head. Logically, you know it's correct. You know you're supposed to do it. It's as good as done. And then, the moment you start talking to her, you feel that sickness in your stomach. Like you swallowed a snake."

The forest trilled and buzzed.

"You thought you could keep them alive," said George, "but you couldn't."

"No," said Hollywood. "You're not listening to me."

He took out a piece of gum and bit into it viciously.

"I don't understand," said George.

"It's not my fault," said Hollywood. "Why does it feel like my fault?"

He'd managed to pull a strip of bark free, and was turning it around in his hands.

"Nobody forced them to sign up for this," said Hollywood. "They were going to do it no matter what."

"Hmm," said George.

Hollywood threw the bark away and pressed knuckles against his eyelids.

"I knew they were going to die," he said, so quietly that George barely heard him.

George closed his eyes and tried to hear the blood pulsing through his temples.

"We go back tomorrow," said Hollywood.

"No."

"Excuse me?"

"You haven't taken me to the forest."

"Where do you think you are, genius? The moon?"

"I mean the real forest. The part that can talk to me."

Hollywood laughed sadly. "I don't know where that is."

"Your brochures—"

"Said we could give you a chance of turning green. If the forest 'chose' you. Which, for all we know, is true. But our whole plan was to drag you out here, traipse around for a few days, then drag you back."

"I'm going to keep looking," said George, eyes stinging.

They listened to the forest move.

"Why?" said Hollywood eventually.

George squeezed blood out of the bug bite and stared into the distant canopy, where the leaves blended together into a deep green paste.

"To say goodbye to my son," he said.

Hollywood stayed quiet for a long time. Eventually he shifted, found a more comfortable seat on the branch, and crossed his arms across his chest.

"There might be a way," he said.

George watched him from the corner of his eye.

"On my very first expedition," said Hollywood, "Tetris and I found something out here."

Far below, a three-story praying mantis picked its way through the undergrowth, oblivious to their presence.

"Since then, I feel a little pull. A tug in the back of my head. It's brought me to monoliths, tablets, pyramids... I could take you. Maybe then, if you got real close, you'd be able to talk to it."

George closed his eyes. Frank, Murlock, Matherson, Bradley, Mitchell, Rosalina and her husband: ribbons of meat. Did he want to end up like that? He thought about the future awaiting him on shore. It was impossible to picture. When he tried, his imagination ran up against a concrete wall.

Somewhere above, a birdlike creature unleashed a string of high, clear notes.

"Take me," said George.

*****

It rained for days, mercilessly, relentlessly, a flood that sorted itself through the leaves and fell in pummeling columns to the forest floor. Hollywood and George didn't exchange a word the whole time. Their ponchos were inadequate. The air hung heavy with moisture, sticking to their skin, pearling along spiderwebs, dripping languidly off the leaves of giant forest plants. Mushrooms sprouted everywhere.

While it rained, the forest slept. They passed the carcass of a scorpion, untouched by scavengers, its stinger draped limply against a fallen tree.

George's skin, perpetually damp, began to itch. He dreamed that it started sloughing off, leaving him a red-muscled freak, his bare eyeballs rolling in their sockets. Still the rain fell. The many intermixing sounds—dull patter, restless leaf-rustle, lurking distant roar—burrowed into his ears, so that he couldn't hear them unless he really focused.

One day, as he passed beneath a thin strand of plummeting rainwater, George slipped on a wet leaf and went sliding toward a chasm. As he scrambled for purchase, hurtling down the slope, a fleshy pink creature heaved itself out of the ravine and opened its mouth to receive him. The creature's eyeless head was rimmed with hundreds of undulating flagella. The throat beyond the mouth was ridged and bottomless. George dug his feet in uselessly, watching the demon-slug grow larger, and then Hollywood came sliding headfirst after him.

The ranger slammed against George's back, wrapping an arm through his harness. They spun, accelerating despite George's frenzied kicks, and then something yanked hard against him: Hollywood had somehow landed a grapple. They leapt skyward, George dangling inches above the blind worm's head. One of his feet kicked a wriggling flagellum, and the beast reacted instantly, lunging into the air.

As the hot, reeking breath enveloped him, George hugged his knees to his chest. For a moment they were inside the worm's mouth. The round lips puckered inward. Just before the aperture closed, Hollywood and George slipped through.

Jaws clamped around nothing but air, the creature fell, pink bulk quivering, into the chasm.

George and Hollywood rested on a branch high above and savored the clean, sweet air.

"Well," said George after a while.

They were drenched in rainwater and slug slime. George scratched his nose.

"I have no fucking clue why I did that," said Hollywood.

George stared at his hands, trying to stop them from

shaking. "I'm glad you did, though."

Hollywood spit off the edge.

"Yeah," he said, "me too."

Two hours later, the rain stopped. They found a branch over a wide ravine, beneath a sparse section of canopy, and lay there sunning themselves. Hollywood stripped to his underwear and spread his clothes out to dry. George followed suit. They stayed there all afternoon, listening to nothing, drinking in the sunlight that filtered through the leaves.

"Do you want to hear a joke?" asked Hollywood.

George shrugged.

"A man has three young daughters," said Hollywood. "One afternoon his oldest comes up with a puzzled look on her face.

"'Daddy,' she says, 'why did you name me Rose?'

"'Well,' he says, 'when you were born, a rose petal drifted down and landed on your head.'"

George watched the leaves rustle through one another.

"The little girl is satisfied by this answer. She skips away. A few minutes later, the next-oldest daughter comes up.

"'Daddy,' she says, 'why did you name me Daisy?'

"'Well,' says the man, 'when you were born, a daisy petal floated over and landed on your head.'"

Hollywood's voice was low and smooth, the contours of the story slipping off his tongue with the ease of endless practice.

"This daughter is satisfied too. She skips away, singing,

curls abounce, et cetera. The father smiles and returns to his newspaper. Before he finishes a paragraph, his youngest daughter comes lumbering around the corner.

"'Ehhhyeearrrghh! Eurnhg Grugggn?' she shouts.

"The man looks at her. 'Shut up, Cinderblock,' he says, and turns the page."

A bug flew into George's mouth. He coughed and spit it out.

"That's pretty good," he said.

Hollywood rolled over to lie on his stomach, chasing a beetle along the side of the branch with a dangling finger. "It's alright."

"Your name's Douglas Douglas, right?"

"Nobody calls me that."

"Well."

On the other side of the canyon, a tarantula made its way down a tree trunk, hairy legs feeling the air. George watched it drowsily, wondering if he could count on Hollywood to stay awake if he slipped into a nap.

"It's an awful name," said Hollywood. "My dad had it out for me from the start."

George closed his eyes. A whisper of undergrowth signaled the passage of some huge creature far below.

"He's a lot like the guys we came in here with," said Hollywood. "Rich. Arrogant. Self-assured."

"Still your dad," said George.

"Nah," said Hollywood.

They lay there, listening, cocooned by tropical heat.

"He disowned me," said Hollywood.

George looked at him for the first time in half an hour. There were scars, huge claw marks, across the ranger's back.

"Why?"

"I backed over his poodle. In the Luxury SUV."

"On purpose?"

"Kind of, yeah."

"Ah."

"Last-straw kind of thing. We'd been fighting for years. Stepmom didn't like me either."

"Hmm," said George, who couldn't imagine disowning a child.

"For the record," said Hollywood, "the poodle deserved it."

*****

They came upon the monolith in a clearing ringed by brilliant beetleflowers. Hollywood refused to approach, but he gestured onward. As George approached, everything seemed to fall silent. He ran his hands along the cool gray surface, the immaculately-edged grooves. After a moment he sank down, closed his eyes, and pressed his ear against it.

The stone was cold. He thought he heard a distant ringing, a jet engine cutting the sky. He felt infinitely old. His muscles, stringy but tough from months of exertion, thrummed.

He thought about his wife. Ex-wife. About Todd. About Thomas. About George Matherson, who'd shared his tent, and Bob Bradley, and Rosalina and her husband, and all the other trainees. His hands trembled. Maybe he was alive because he didn't fear death. Maybe that was the secret. He didn't welcome it, exactly, but he didn't think he'd mind, either. He'd given life a good try.

He missed so many people. He missed people he'd only met once or twice, like his uncle Rob, who'd turned him upside down at age seven and spun him around by his heels. Rob, whose first wife had convinced him to get a vasectomy, then left him when the procedure went horribly wrong. Whose second wife had not-so-secretly wanted kids. Rob, who himself had loved kids. Rob, who at forty-five had stuck a shotgun in his mouth and—

Every story George could think of terminated in tragedy. But for some reason, sitting here one hundred miles from the nearest non-Hollywood human being, enveloped in esurient jungle, with insects lighting on his neck to drink his sweat, that didn't seem so sad. It seemed natural. Every story ultimately ended in death. So why worry about it? It was like worrying about the sun coming up.

He listened. The monolith was cold and still and silent.

Thoughts rattled around his head. He was disintegrating. The parts of his mind that defined him were tearing apart, revealing glistening thought-filaments packed with memories and dreams, regrets and hatreds and fears. Fiber-optic neural strands surged with electric-blue energy.

Here he was. The gray fog obscuring his future had begun to clear. Sunbeams pierced the clouds. Deep inside, he felt a kernel of hope. Hope for what, exactly, he couldn't say. Something different. As different as a man his age could expect. Maybe he'd go to school. Study engineering. Start over from scratch.

Or maybe he'd just sit here, ear against the cold stone, and keep his eyes closed, and wait for something to consume him.

Either option was fine.

18

Hollywood waited as long as he could, and then, when he saw that George had dozed off, he took a deep breath, squared his pack on his shoulders, and marched into the clearing. The humming in his head intensified, but he set his eyes straight, step-step-stepped into range, grabbed George under the shoulders, and dragged him away.

Once he was far enough that the cerebral buzzing had subsided to bearable levels, Hollywood slapped George's face, but the older man only groaned and turned his head from side to side. Adrenaline spiking, Hollywood lifted the inert body over his shoulders and jogged, knees creaking. His back hurt. The forest roared and rustled around him. He crossed a hundred yards and grapple-gunned into the branches.

The elevation seemed to help. After a moment or two, George stirred, blinking as if waking for the first time in years.

Hollywood held up a canteen. "Hey. Hey. You alright?"

George, an incandescent grin splitting his face: "He's alive."

"Say again?"

"My son's alive."

Hollywood sighed.

"It showed me," said George.

"It showed me lots of shit," said Hollywood. "None of it came true."

They turned back. One day they were crossing a fallen tree that lay across a ravine when Hollywood, uncharacteristically distracted, slipped and went over the edge. As he fell, he spun, grasping at splinters of bark, and it crystallized that he was about to die in the most embarrassing possible way. Then George caught his arm.

That night Hollywood dreamed that a giant horned moth picked him up and carried him through the canopy and over the forest. A thousand miles of rolling green passed beneath them, the wind a cold sheet wrapped around his face.

Hollywood asked the moth: "Where are you taking

me?"

And the moth replied: "Back to where you started."

But Hollywood could tell from the position of the chalky moon that they were headed west, deeper into the Pacific, not toward the shore. Before he could ask the moth what it meant, a mountain rose out of the forest. The misty green peak blasted all thoughts from his mind.

*****

Zip watched a documentary series on the trains and superhighways spanning the polar wastes. The series was an effort to make the frozen north as intriguing and adventurous as the forest—an attempt, in other words, to replicate the tremendous commercial success of the ranger programs with significantly lower overhead. Unfortunately, the polar wastes were by definition boring, endless stretches of tundra broken only by the occasional malnourished polar bear. Journeys across the expanse, except in the case of mechanical failure, were by-and-large uneventful. Nor were the people who worked the wastes particularly interesting. Rangers tended to have big personalities. Polar waste workers were taciturn misanthropes who'd chosen their profession specifically to get away from other human beings.

He watched the whole series anyway. He couldn't stand the ranger programs, and nothing else was anywhere near as entertaining. He tried and failed to read books. Rock climbing, his original passion, now only infuriated him. Routes that would once have been trivial were now impossible. He spent hours on his apartment balcony, watching people walk by. Lots of them were ugly. Sometimes he'd go all day without seeing a beautiful one.

The sky was always gray. When it wasn't gray it was white. When it wasn't white or gray it was black, and rain fell out of it. But it was never blue.

Hollywood didn't come back when he said he would. Zip stayed in his apartment. When he thought about things to do, they all sounded awful, so he didn't do anything. Doing nothing felt awful too. It was the same with food: nothing sounded appetizing, so he ate whatever was easiest, potato chips and fast food and cans of soup. The days dragged on, and still Hollywood failed to appear.

One day, Zip called his mother and talked to her for a long time. Then he dropped the phone on the floor and lay on his back in the living room, counting dimples in the stucco ceiling.

The best metaphor for how he felt was that he was trapped in a cloud of black flies. When he opened his mouth they flowed inside and he had to spit them out. Their bodies crunched and oozed between his molars. Trying to spit simply let more flies inside, their wings adhering to the roof of his mouth, so at last he had to swallow. It was no use shouting for help, because the buzz drowned out every sound.

When he couldn't stand it anymore, he put on his sneakers and drove to the nearest state park.

It was the middle of the week and the park was

deserted. He picked a trail that led to a cliff and set off at once. It didn't take long to realize that he'd forgotten a water bottle. His sweatshirt and jeans became a sweltering, swampy prison. He tied the sweatshirt around his waist, but sweat still poured hot and fast down his face.

The trail was rough. After half a mile, the dirt path metamorphosed into uneven stone steps. He struggled up, his prosthetic leg stiff, the unwieldy foot with its worn-out sneaker sliding around and twice sending him crashing down. His elbows and knee turned bright red and bled. He stuck a pebble in his mouth to fend off the thirst.

He passed a bush that rustled menacingly, but kept on going, prompting a rattlesnake to burst out and strike his prosthetic leg. Pink-webbed fangs glanced off. Undeterred, the snake struck again, but the prosthetic leg repelled the fangs. Zip stood still, breathing through his nose. The snake coiled and hissed, tail jittering. Zip picked up a big rock. The snake watched him.

"Hisssssssssss," it said.

"Fuck off," said Zip.

The rock was a satisfying weight in his hand. Half of his brain said: kill the snake. Look at its mean fucking eyes. The other half said: don't kill it. It's just scared. Look at its beautiful scales. Look at those gold and brown diamonds.

He closed his eyes and tasted the sweet air, rolling the pebble around in his mouth. Then he extended his prosthetic, baiting another strike. When the snake fell for the trick, fangs rebounding uselessly, Zip obliterated its head. It took a couple blows, and when the snake stopped moving Zip felt so nauseous that he had to drop the rock and stagger away. He tried to throw up behind a tree, but he hadn't eaten anything that morning, so the retches brought up nothing at all.

The trees were a tenth the size of forest trees, but they still towered above him. He watched the ground, not the sky, as he fought his way up the mountain. Birds laughed and taunted with their cries. A chunk of stone crumbled away as he stepped on it, and he fell, body weight landing on his prosthetic leg, which snapped at the shin. He tried to take another few steps, licking sour, chapped lips, but the leg kept buckling under him. He found a stick to prop himself up and continued up the slope.

Eventually he came to a stream, which cascaded down a series of steps to his left and crossed the trail before vanishing into the forest. He lapped up water as it trickled down. It tasted clear and pure. He gulped down mouthfuls, blinking as drops clung to his eyelashes.

Something round and smooth touched his tongue and he spat. A tadpole, expelled, writhed on the gravelly trail. Zip tried to brush it back into the stream, but its sensitive belly split open on the rough stones, leaving a trail of guts and blood. The nausea swelled again. Zip distracted himself by looking upstream.

A few stair-steps above, the stream pattered across a broad-leafed plant painted white and black with bird feces.

Zip spat and rubbed his tongue on his sleeve. His

mouth tasted foul. He spat again and swore, hauling himself up. Stupid. His stomach hurt. It had to be his imagination. You couldn't get sick that fast.

He dragged himself up the slope, worthless prosthetic leg buckling, the gnarled walking stick barely keeping him upright. It felt like he'd been walking for hours. He would have checked his phone to see the exact time, but he'd forgotten it in the car. He spat into the undergrowth again and again, but the taste remained.

Zip wasn't sure why it was so important that he reached the top of the trail. He stumped along, leaning on the stick, grunting with every step. The broken prosthetic dug into his stump. He was pretty sure he was bleeding down there, but he refused to stop and take a look. His good leg's muscles screamed.

When Tetris and Li had showed up in D.C., if he'd gone to see them immediately, would they still have gotten on that plane? Would he have gone too? Would he be dead now?

Why hadn't he gone? He'd stayed at home, watching them on the television screen.

Everything had gone to shit since he'd lost the leg.

Although. Now that he really thought about it—he settled onto a mossy rock to give his aching joints a rest— he hadn't really been happy before he lost it, either. Spikes of happiness, sure. There'd been times in the forest, with Tetris and Li, that he'd felt normal. And he was pretty sure he'd always maintained a convincing illusion of happiness. To conceal the buzzing flies. Maybe he'd even managed to delude himself.

His left eye itched, so he rubbed it, but the itching only intensified. He squinted at his fingers. They were dirty. He tried to find a clean scrap of clothing or skin to rub his eye on, but everything was covered in dirt. Finally he turned up his shirt and rubbed a section of sweaty interior against his eye. It stung, but the itching stopped.

What was he planning on doing when he reached the cliff?

Zip closed his eyes and conjured the scene in the forest. He'd stood on a flimsy branch above the spider, brazen, firing his worthless pistol. Why? It could have climbed up after him. He should have grappled away. But he stayed.

Was it possible that the rage he'd felt when he woke in the branches had not been directed at his injuries, or at Tetris and Li for risking their lives, but at his failure to—

Well. He hadn't really wanted to kill the rattlesnake, either, had he?

His gashes sang. Afterward there would be no pain, only silence. Would that be any better?

He removed his prosthetic and examined the place where it had cracked. Imagined sitting on the edge of the cliff, looking over the lumpy treetops, the mountain rising against the gray sky to his left. He imagined the breeze kissing his sweaty cheeks. He imagined slipping as he turned to leave, tumbling over the edge, the seconds of orgasmic flight before swift sharp pain and then nothing.

He sat and listened to the birds for a long time. A ladybug landed on his arm and he left it there. The forest around him was extremely green. The air tasted nice.

Well, there was no rush. He reattached the prosthetic, grabbed his walking stick, and hobbled down the mountain.

When he got back to his apartment, poured a glass of water, and sank into his armchair, Chomper orbiting his leg, Zip noticed a missed call on his phone.

Hollywood.

He'd listen to the voicemail in a second. For now, all he wanted to do was sit, drink his water, and scratch Chomper on the spot beneath his collar where he best liked to be scratched.

19

When Zip opened the door to Hollywood's office, he found the blond ranger sweeping the contents of a mahogany desk into cardboard boxes. The bookshelf along the wall had been gutted, as had the wall with various fake awards printed and framed by Hollywood himself.

"Hey," said Hollywood, wiping sweat from his crooked nose.

"Packing up?"

"Just canceled all the expeditions and the office lease."

Zip kicked a stress relief ball. It flew across the room and molded around a leg of the desk.

"At least we got a nice payout, right?" said Hollywood, and laughed. Zip thought it sounded a bit forced.

"Where's George?"

"He wandered off," said Hollywood. "Before you chew me out: he didn't leave empty-handed. I gave him fifty thousand bucks."

"You let him leave? Also, what? That's nothing."

"What was I supposed to do? Handcuff him? I'd say we left him significantly better off than we found him."

Zip fingered a drawstring on his hoodie. Someone tapped the wall and cleared their throat behind him.

"Excuse me," said a man in the hallway, in a lilting accent Zip didn't recognize, "would this happen to be the office of Forest Adventuring Travels, LLC?"

"Sorry, bud," said Hollywood, trying to figure out how to fit a massive three-hole-punch into a box already brimming with supplies, "we here at FAT just closed our doors. Not accepting new customers."

The man, who barely came up to Zip's shoulder, squeezed his eyes in a vaguely avian approximation of a smile. "Oh, but I am not a customer. I am an attorney. I represent a foreign client who would like to retain your capabilities for a unique, one-time engagement."

He bustled past Zip, extending a business card to Hollywood. Light glinted off gold lettering.

"This is just a phone number," observed Hollywood.

"My client values discretion," said the man.

"Whatever you're buying, I don't sell it," said

Hollywood, and tossed the card in the trash.

The man's eyes followed the card's flight. His mouth remained open for a moment. Then he reached into his pocket and produced another card. This one he held up like a dog treat.

"My client," said the man, waving the card, "will reward you handsomely for your service."

Hollywood snorted. "I just pulled down twenty million dollars," he said. "You can't buy me."

"One expedition. Fifty million dollars, each."

Hollywood froze with a stapler halfway to the box.

"Think about it," said the man, laying the card on the desk. He extended a hand for a shake. Hollywood looked at it like it was a bloody stump. After a moment the hand withdrew.

"Good day," said the man, and departed.

"Absolutely not," said Zip.

"Absolutely FIFTY MILLION DOLLARS," said Hollywood.

"You're already rich. You said it yourself."

"Not rich enough. Fifty million dollars—Zip, with that kind of money—"

"Then do it. Without me."

"Zip. Please. They're not going to take you into the forest. Show up, train another batch of suckers, take your check, and adios. C'mon, man! It's a no-brainer!"

Zip kneaded his forehead.

"Listen to me, Zip. My father is a jackass.

Unfortunately he is also a millionaire. Except for killing his insufferable poodle, I have never been able to give him even the tiniest spoonful of the dastardly comeuppance he so desperately deserves."

"What does fifty million do that twenty million doesn't?"

"I'm getting to that. My father lives next to another jackass millionaire, whose equally preposterous fortune stems from the fact that he invented the moist towelette. Every time you swab your mouth, typically at a restaurant with 'Shack' in its name, this guy gets a cut. If I had fifty million dollars, I would buy the Moist Towelette Tyrant's property. And do you know what I would build there? I would erect, Zip, on the plot of land directly adjacent to my father's, a towering golden phallus the likes of which the world has never seen. A ten-story, tumescent wiener, piercing the very heavens, glistening gold, bulging with veins. Imagine!"

Zip nodded. "I'm imagining."

"No you're—you're not, I can tell by your face. I can tell that you're not."

"I am. I really am. A giant metal penis, is what you're saying. This isn't a fucking M.C. Escher you're trying to—

"Zip! A macro-dong of obscene proportions! The turgid, empyrean majesty! Can't you feel it?"

Zip gave up. "Okay. I feel it."

"Surely there's something you'd do with fifty million dollars."

"I'd give a couple million to each of my parents," said

Zip, "so they'd finally divorce each other."

Hollywood gaped. "You are one depressing guy, huh?"

Zip scratched the beard that had begun accumulating along his jawline. "I'd also get a blimp."

"Cruise liner? Aircraft carrier? Luxury speedliner? What kind of airship are we talking, here, captain?"

"Something modest."

"No. Nooooo. This is not the occasion for modesty. We are talking about fifty million dollars, Zip."

"Jeez, man, you know how much an airship costs? Gotta be five million just for a little one."

"It's free money! Splurge!"

"I'd buy a big fucking airship and paint a pin-up girl on the side. Is that what you want me to say?"

"Her tits hanging out. Yeah. I could see that."

"No, I mean, in a bikini? Because I'm not a weirdo?"

Hollywood tapped his chin. "I see what you're going for. My opinion, though, you'd really want her to be full-on nude. For artistic effect."

Zip, over his growling stomach: "I'll take that under advisement."

"Shit," said Hollywood, checking his oversized watch, "it's two o'clock. Pizza?"

So they went to Pete's Pizza Shack and demolished an extra-large pie with all the toppings. When they were done they wiped their faces with lemon-scented moist towelettes.

On the sidewalk, Hollywood fished out the business card. Zip, teetering on the edge of a food coma, watched sunlight play off the golden script.

"You in?" asked Hollywood.

"I honestly don't know," said Zip.

"Tell you what," said Hollywood, putting the card between his teeth and digging for his wallet. He held out a quarter and motioned.

After a second, Zip took the quarter.

"Heads you go," said Hollywood, "tails you don't."

Zip flipped the coin. It caught the sun on its way up, and he had to look away. When he turned back, the coin was rolling down the sidewalk, bouncing on its edge. It hopped off the curb and vanished through a sewer grate.

"What's that mean?" asked Zip.

"It means you owe me a quarter," said Hollywood, the phone already pressed against his ear.

Three days later they were standing together in the airport security line, Hollywood with gigantic aviators on his face and a chunk of bubble gum popping in his mouth, Zip lugging the same beat-up suitcase he'd brought to boot camp five years earlier.

"They'll take me aside for a pat down," said Zip, "just you watch."

Hollywood peered over his aviators. "Nah, man, you're black, not Muslim. It's the Ay-rabs they're after."

"Look at this beard. Plus the prosthetic. I could have a bomb in there. I bet you a million bucks."

"Whoa. Shake on that?"

They shook.

"That guy's a racist," said Zip, motioning with his head.

"Like, more than usual, I mean. I can tell."

Hollywood looked. A group of TSA officers socialized beside the X-Ray machine. "The fat one?"

"The one with the beady little eyes. The goatee. Look, he's staring. If that fucker doesn't have a Confederate flag on his pick-up truck, I'll eat a bucket of pig slop."

"God bless America," said Hollywood, sizing up a buxom blonde as she bent to remove her shoes. "You seeing her, though?"

"Hmm," said Zip.

"I'd hit that so hard it would orbit the Sun," said Hollywood.

"That doesn't—that doesn't make any sense."

"Halley's Comet that hoe."

"It's amazing you managed to mispronounce that word."

"'Halley?'"

"No. Never mind."

"What—how am I supposed to say it, then?"

"Don't," said Zip, producing his boarding pass. "Just don't."

"See," said Hollywood, "*that's* racism."

The TSA officials couldn't figure out why Zip laughed when they asked him to step aside for a pat down, so they put him in a little room for a few minutes and searched his luggage. When he emerged, Hollywood greeted him with a shrug.

"Easiest one million dollars of my young life," said Zip.

"While you were in there I came up with a great rap

line," said Hollywood.

"No," said Zip. "Please, no."

"Slam that hoe so hard that she orbits the sun—"

"God, no—stop. Please stop."

"—they be call her Hailey's Comet by the time I is done."

"Holy shit, Hollywood."

"Get it? Like, 'Hailey?' Like the name?"

"Did you honestly say 'they be call her?' Is that what you said?"

"It was for flow. Flow, man. Look, I know all about this stuff. I'm a hip hop head."

"Oh my God."

"I listen to Outkast, man! I listen to Kanye!"

"Oh my God."

"I'm practically as black as you are, Zachary."

Zip put a hand on his shoulder.

"Douglas," he said, "you are so white that you not only have the whitest name imaginable, you have it twice."

"There are plenty of black guys named Douglas," said Hollywood.

"On top of that, Douglas, you are nicknamed after a place that is notorious for being full of white people."

"Did you not see that Tarantino movie? The one about the slave?"

"Douglas, you are the whitest person I know. You are whiter than Tetris, which is saying something, because Tetris is an Indiana trailer park boy."

"Well, he's green, actually. Not white."

"You are whiter than Twinkie filling, Douglas."

"Was, I mean," said Hollywood.

"What?"

"Tetris *was* green."

Zip closed his mouth. His suitcase wheels growled against the tile. A lady came over the intercom, loud and unintelligible.

"I forget sometimes," Zip said after a while.

"Yeah," said Hollywood. "I get that."

*****

Zip and Hollywood had seats in first class, but a trip from Seattle to Portugal was still a trip from Seattle to Portugal, and with a four hour layover in Philadelphia it added up to seventeen consecutive hours of travel. Half an hour into the first flight, it was clear that Hollywood's strategy to cope was to get utterly shit-faced on tiny bottles of airplane liquor. Zip, who'd won the rock-paper-scissors match for the window seat, watched the checkered green and brown plains of the Midwest roll by. Eventually he acquiesced to Hollywood's repeated and importunate demands that he partake in the free alcohol, and downed a miniature bottle of whiskey himself. Then another. Things went downhill from there.

When they staggered off the plane in Philadelphia, arms around each other's shoulders, the world looked a whole lot brighter. They stood, swaying, obstructing the entrance to the boarding tunnel, oblivious to the mob of passengers struggling to squeeze by.

"I want a smoothie," announced Zip.

"Me too," said Hollywood.

They bought smoothies. Five minutes passed in silence.

"You know what I want?" said Hollywood. "An iPod."

He tried to drop his half-full smoothie into a trash can and missed. The cup hit the ground and ruptured, strawberry goop splorting out in an alluvial pink fan.

"Whoops," said Zip, and laughed.

Hollywood snorted. "I did not mean to do that."

They wandered the airport, riding the moving walkways, in search of a vending machine with electronics. Eventually they found one. It took Hollywood several minutes to decipher the touchscreen menu, but in the end he purchased an iPod. Several iPods, in fact. They came raining down into the collection slot like square white missiles.

"Man," said Zip, "what are you going to do with eleven iPods?"

"Help me hold them," said Hollywood, taking the boxes out of the slot and passing them over. Zip's arms were quickly filled. Hollywood pulled Zip's roller bag, and Zip carried the teetering pile of iPods. He didn't do a very good job. They were down to six by the time they reached the gate.

"Shit," said Zip, "I must have dropped a bunch."

Hollywood didn't look particularly upset. He turned a box over in his hands, trying to figure out how to open it.

Suddenly his fingers froze.

"Wait," he said, "how am I going to get music onto this?"

Zip shrugged. "I didn't even know they still *made* iPods."

Horror spread across Hollywood's face. "I don't even *want* an iPod."

A TSA agent walked by, arms stacked with the five missing iPod boxes.

"Hey," said Hollywood, lunging to his feet. "Those are mine!"

"Hollywood, no," shouted Zip, staggering after him.

"Give those back," bellowed Hollywood, accelerating to a clumsy sprint.

Startled by the slap of their footsteps, the TSA agent turned. For a moment his eyes went wide. Then Hollywood tackled him, and Zip tackled Hollywood, and the three of them hit the ground, iPods jettisoned in all directions, and Zip began to realize, as a shouting horde of officers came running, that they probably weren't going to make it to Portugal today after all.

*****

"Officer," said Hollywood, "this is all a huge misunderstanding."

"I heard you the first time," said the officer, his feet up on the desk, as he worked his way through the Sports section of the Philadelphia Tribune.

Zip, on the bunk in the back of the cell, sighed and rubbed the spots on his wrists where the cuffs had dug in.

"Honestly, I think it was a blatant case of racial profiling, because of my friend here," said Hollywood, pointing at Zip. "You'd probably know all about that, right?"

The officer slowly turned his head. "Excuse me?"

"I mean, because you're black. You probably get racially profiled all the time."

"Hollywood," said Zip.

"Doesn't it bother you? To see a couple of guys locked up for no reason except racism? Doesn't that hurt, somewhere deep in your black heart?"

The officer put his newspaper down and rose from his chair.

"No, wait, no. No no no," said Hollywood, "that's not what I meant. 'Black heart' as in: black-hearted, you know? Not as in: because you are black. Ha! Whoops. Black-hearted! It's a saying!"

"I told you," rumbled the officer, "to stop talking."

Hollywood snorted. "This is America, man. I know my rights."

"Hollywood," said Zip.

The police officer's nostrils flared. He raised a finger the diameter of a rifle barrel and opened his mouth. Then the station's double doors swung open, revealing the diminutive attorney they'd met in Hollywood's office.

"Alright," said the attorney, "let them out."

Three tight-jawed policemen entered after him.

"What?" said the officer by their cell.

"I already explained this to several dozen of your colleagues. No one is pressing charges. It is your legal imperative to release my clients."

"They assaulted a law enforcement officer," said the towering policeman, stabbing his index finger in Hollywood's direction.

"Allegedly," said the attorney primly. "Now let them out, please."

Outside, Zip hurried to catch the attorney. "How'd you get us off the hook?"

"The individual you attacked," said the attorney, "decided not to press charges."

"Just like that?"

The attorney glanced over. "Upon a thorough investigation, the TSA opted to let the incident slide."

They headed towards a black Lincoln.

"We rebooked your flight," said the attorney as he ducked into the shotgun seat. "I will be accompanying you to forestall any further complications."

He meant it. When they boarded the plane, and Hollywood asked the stewardess for a nightcap, the attorney cleared his throat and stared him down.

"Fine," said Hollywood, and pouted for two hours, until finally he succumbed to exhaustion and fell asleep.

The attorney, who still hadn't mentioned his name, saw them personally to their hotel in Lisbon. It was afternoon in Portugal, the sun dangling above tiers of orange-roofed buildings.

"I will return at seven o'clock tomorrow morning to retrieve you," said the attorney. "Can I trust that you will refrain from further trouble-making in the interim?"

"Man," said Hollywood, "what's your problem?"

The attorney bristled. "If it were up to me, we would never have solicited your participation in the first place. Rest assured that I continue to make frequent and impassioned arguments for your termination. All of which is to say, if you insist on acting like children, sirs, expect to be treated like children."

"Eat a dick," said Zip.

"How eloquent," said the attorney, and climbed back into the car.

In the morning he drove them across the city, whizzing through narrow white-walled alleys, rattling up slopes and flying down hills. For a reserved man, he drove like a maniac, but it was a controlled kind of madness, the aggression moderated by quick reflexes and manic precision. When a truck careened out of an alley in front of them, the attorney whipped their car into the opposite lane, gunned the engine, and swung them back into the original lane just in time for another car to hurtle past in the opposite direction. The whole maneuver happened so quickly that Zip hardly had time to register the near-collision. Nor did the attorney react in any way to the superhuman feat he'd just performed.

They came to a stodgy gray building on the far side of Lisbon. Zip and Hollywood followed the attorney to the front door, echoing each others' yawns.

"Please behave," said the attorney, and led the way.

On the other side of the door stood the buxom blonde from the airport security line.

"Holy shit," said Hollywood.

"Hi," she said, unveiling a six thousand-lumen smile. "It's nice to meet you. My name is Hailey Sumner."

"Holy shit," said Zip.

"I trust Mr. Terpsichorean has been taking care of you?"

It took Zip a minute to realize she was talking about the attorney.

"Uh," he said.

"For God's sake," said Mr. Terpsichorean.

"He's a bundle of laughs," said Hollywood.

"Fantastic," said Sumner, tossing her hair back and shaking Hollywood's hand. "Sorry about the inconveniences in Philadelphia."

They followed her down an unmarked hallway and into a conference room with padded leather chairs.

"What is this place?" asked Zip.

"Take a seat," said Sumner, "and I'll get you up to speed."

Zip settled dubiously into one of the voluminous chairs.

"It may not look like much," said Sumner, "but these are the headquarters of the Omphalos Initiative."

"Never heard of it," said Hollywood.

"That's because it's secret."

"Okay. It's just that, the way you said it, you kind of—

it sounded like you expected me to know what it was."

"Well," said Sumner, smiling patiently, "I didn't."

"Great. Good. Got it."

"Do you want to know—"

"What the Oompa-Loompa Institute does? Sure. But first I have a more important question."

The smile slipped off Sumner's face. She tapped a pen on the table. "Go ahead."

"Want to grab a drink tonight?" asked Hollywood.

The room was very quiet. Mr. Terpsichorean expelled all the air from his lungs in a single explosive burst.

"I do not," said Sumner curtly. All traces of the smile had vanished. "The Omphalos Initiative is an international organization supported by a worldwide network of powerful donors. Our goal is to help humanity reach the next stage of evolution by merging with the World Forest."

"Okay," said Hollywood, "I get that. I get that. I see where you're coming from. Is it because I was too forward? Or do you not find me attractive."

"Mr. Douglas," hissed the attorney.

Sumner tilted her head. "Around here, Mr. Douglas, behavior like that will not be tolerated. Do I make myself clear?"

In her blue-flecked eyes, Zip saw a glint of something he didn't like at all.

Hollywood straightened. "I'm just messing around, ma'am."

"I am not," she said, placing each word deliberately,

"someone with whom you wish to mess around."

"I think I'd like to speak to your boss," said Hollywood.

Faster than a striking viper, Sumner's smile returned.

"Unfortunately for you," she said, "I am the boss."

Hollywood frowned. "Oh."

"Yes. 'Oh.'"

Mr. Terpsichorean looked like he was about to faint.

"I would like to retain your services," said Sumner, "but rest assured, if you prove to be a dissatisfactory partner, I will find an alternative."

"I understand," said Hollywood. Zip felt like laughing and crying at the same time.

"Mr. Douglas," said Sumner, "how long does it typically take one of your expeditions to reach an electromagnetic anomaly?"

Hollywood gaped.

"Mr. Douglas?"

"Uh. Well, it usually—we're usually out there for about two weeks."

"I don't understand. What do you mean, 'usually?' Do the anomalies move?"

"Ah," said Hollywood, "I don't—when you say anomaly, do you mean—"

Sumner raised her immaculate eyebrows. "If you don't even know what an anomaly is, how on Earth do your clients hope to achieve transcendence?"

Zip snorted.

Sumner swiveled. "Mr. Chase?"

"Ma'am," said Zip, "with all due respect, we're just tour

guides. We take wealthy suckers out and walk them around. That's it."

He struggled to meet her blistering stare.

She pressed three fingertips on the table. "It appears that Mr. Terpsichorean was correct. You're a couple of con men."

"We're a couple of rangers," said Hollywood.

"You don't know anything at all."

"Ma'am," said Hollywood, "I know as much about the forest as anyone alive. My physical condition is impeccable. My tactical poise is peerless. If it's a guide you need, I have all the necessary qualifications."

"You have a big fucking mouth, is what you have," said Sumner.

"Look," said Zip, "we thought you needed a trainer and a guide. If that's not what you need, we're happy to get out of your hair. No harm done. Give us a week and we'll forget all about the Ompalooze Imbroglio."

"Omphalos Initiative," snapped Sumner. Zip scratched his nose. All of a sudden Sumner smoothed her face out.

"There's another way," she said.

"Ms. Sumner," said Mr. Terpsichorean sharply, "it's far too risky."

"Maybe not," she said.

"It," said Mr. Terpsichorean, face contorted as if in response to a horrible taste, "is too unpredictable."

"We can regulate that. Have regulated that."

"Hello?" said Hollywood. "Forget we were here?"

Sumner's gaze snapped back to him. She stood. "Come

with me."

"Where?" demanded Hollywood.

But she was already on her way out the door.

As they strode down the hall, Sumner blasted a stream of words over her shoulder.

"Rapid healing. Photosynthesis. Immunity to all disease. Telepathic communication. Functional immortality. These are the gifts of transcendence. By merging with the forest, a human being can reach an entirely new plane of existence."

"And you think you figured out how to do that," said Zip.

"I don't think," said Sumner. "I know."

They rode an elevator several stories down. Sumner led them along yet another unmarked hallway. Here and there they passed other people, subordinates in curious black-and-green uniforms, but no one made eye contact or spoke to Sumner. They practically pressed themselves against the wall when she passed.

"What makes you so sure?" asked Zip.

They came to a section of hallway lined with tall steel doors. Armed guards stood at attention in front of every second or third entryway. Ignoring them, Sumner tapped a code into a keypad, and a door slid open.

"See for yourself," she said.

The room beyond was small and dark. A floor-to-ceiling window, which Zip took to be a one-way mirror, looked out over a concrete cell. Inside the cell, there was a toilet, a cot, and a small steel desk. The desk and the cot were bolted to the floor.

In the center of the cell, staring up at them with molar-grinding hatred, sat Tetris Aphelion, cross-legged, crackling with pent-up fury, a gray collar fitted around his thick green neck.

20

"Holy shit," said Zip, hands behind his head as he paced the hotel room.

"Fuck," said Hollywood from the armchair.

"Fuck," said Zip.

"Holy shit," said Hollywood.

"That was Tetris!"

"Did you see all those guns?"

"We have to get him out of there. What about Li? Is Li in there? What happened to her?"

"We are so fucked," moaned Hollywood.

"Yeah, you made sure of that, huh? Couldn't keep your fucking mouth shut."

"How was I supposed to know she was a supervillain? How was I even supposed to know she was in charge?"

"What, because she's a woman?"

"No, dude," said Hollywood, exasperated, "because she's a *babe*."

Zip parted the blinds and peered out. Tetris was alive. For now.

"How do we get him out of there?"

"Forget Tetris," said Hollywood, "what are *we* going to do?"

"What's wrong with you?"

"The unarmed ranger and his one-legged sidekick stage an elaborate jailbreak. Real fucking likely."

"Man," said Zip, "you know they're torturing him. How else did they get that information? You think he gave it up because they asked nicely?"

"Alright, then, boss," said Hollywood, "what do you suggest? You saw the guards. Those guys are not fucking around. Kevlar! P90s! Night vision goggles! That's part of their protocol, by the way. Cut the lights if there's an intruder. So we need guns, one, and night vision goggles, two... and a way to get through all the locked doors... and a place to hide for the rest of our miserable fucking lives afterward, because they KNOW WHO WE ARE, and KNOW WHERE WE LIVE, and I don't know if you noticed, Zip, but they appear to be PRETTY WELL FUNDED, since they're paying us a hundred million for one lousy trip!"

Zip ran a hand along his jaw.

"Well?" said Hollywood. "Any bright ideas?"

"We have to try," said Zip.

Hollywood snorted. "Be still, my heart."

"We have the element of surprise."

"Right. We'll just run in there with our dicks out, brandishing our element of surprise."

"We play along. Listen to what they have to say. Get them to trust us, and look for an opening."

"What if there is no opening?"

"What do you want me to say? If we leave him, he'll die."

"What makes you think they won't let him go the moment they grow another green person?"

"I don't know, man. Maybe the fact that they were psychotic enough to imprison him in the first place?"

*****

The recruits Zip was expected to train had little in common with his previous batch. Eight white males between the ages of twenty-five and thirty, in peak physical condition, they paid him unflinching attention as he stumbled through an introductory speech. Their stares unnerved him. He fastened his eyes above their heads and told them to run five laps, which they did, effortlessly. He told them to do a hundred push-ups, then gave them five more laps. No one voiced a complaint. He kept them at it all afternoon.

The next day they went to a grapple-gun course. The trainees attacked the challenge with fervor. They'd clearly been practicing ahead of time. Zip began to wonder how he would fill the weeks to come.

He wondered if the trainees knew about the prisoners. Maybe some of them had tortured Tetris themselves.

"Mr. Chase," said one of the recruits, "we've heard conflicting instructions for what to do when confronted by a tarantula. Are you supposed to stand very still, or are you supposed to run away?"

Your only chance is to try a grapple, thought Zip, because the spider will find you by your heartbeat.

He surveyed the hard faces of the trainees. He imagined them standing stock-still as a tarantula approached, pawing the air with its hairy legs. Imagined the horror when the spider folded one of them up. How could he wish that fate on someone? But then he thought of Tetris, alone in his cell, scarred from months of torture.

"Stand still," said Zip. "That goes for a lot of big things. They'll catch you if you try to flee. So stand perfectly still and hope they don't notice."

He dismissed the class early and walked back to the hotel with a smoldering satisfaction in his belly.

*****

One of the trainees was a freckled twenty-something American named James. The others were various persuasions of European, sporting diverse but uniformly heavy accents. James, who it turned out had grown up a few towns down the road from Zip, spoke with an earnest Southern twang. Like the others, he was in peak physical condition, although overall he was a bit smaller than average, around Zip's height. Unlike the others, who treated Zip with the careful deference reserved for authority figures of uncertain temperament, James was warm and conversational.

One evening after training, James stayed late, pestering Zip with questions. A tuft of hair stuck off the back of his head and wiggled whenever he nodded, which happened a lot. Thirty minutes passed. Just as it occurred to Zip that he was actually enjoying the company of an Omphalos Initiate, James slapped a hand against his worry-crinkled forehead.

"What's wrong?" asked Zip.

"It's my mom's birthday," said James. "I was going to meet her for dinner, but it's my night to feed the prisoners."

A thrill coursed down Zip's spine.

"I can handle that for you," he said. His voice sounded like it was being broadcast back to him through a long cardboard tube.

"Could you?"

"I'm not sure where the prisoners are kept, and I'm not sure my card key gets me access, but..."

"Hell, you can borrow my card. Go to the mess—you know where the mess is, right?—and ask the cook. Eduardo, I think. Take the tray down to B3-11. It's the sixth door on the left."

Zip forced himself to stay very still. "B3-11. Got it." His carefully crafted nonchalance disintegrated when James gave a vapid grin and turned to leave without handing over the access card. "Hey. Hey! Forgetting something?"

James slapped his forehead again. "Sorry about that."

Zip's fingers closed around the card. "Have a good night, man."

He waited, watching the sun splat against the horizon, until James's car vanished from sight. Then he sprinted to his SUV, tossed his bag on the passenger-side floor, and cranked the key in the ignition.

It took Franciscan restraint not to drive like a maniac. Finally an opening. It had been weeks without a sighting of Tetris, but now there was a chance.

He jittered through the front door of Omphalos headquarters—it took him five tries to get the card swipe right—and sauntered down the hall to the cafeteria. Well, tried to saunter, anyway. He was newly aware of his prosthetic leg's inflexibility. Was it always this awkward when he walked? Did people notice?

In the cafeteria he found a tray stacked with prepackaged dinners. The label read "B3-11." No sign of Eduardo. Grateful for the chef's absence, Zip grabbed the tray and slipped out.

The elevator moved much slower than usual. As it descended, it released a slight metallic groan. The doors opened with a hiss.

Heart pounding, Zip traversed the hallway, which smelled like industrial cleaners and fresh-polished steel. The guards he passed nodded when they saw him. Somehow he managed to nod back. Didn't they wonder what an unfamiliar face was doing here? He wasn't even in uniform.

At last he came to the cell. Guards on either side sized him up, then returned to drilling ocular holes in the opposite wall.

"Food for the prisoners," Zip said.

The leftmost guard raised an insouciant hand.

Zip waited. A rivulet of sweat trickled down his neck and curled into his armpit. From there he could feel it dripping to his elbow. His missing leg was kicking up phantom pain again. The prosthetic was itchy and tough against his sweaty stump.

At last the door opened. To Zip's absolute gibbering horror, Hailey Sumner walked out. She closed the door behind her, turned, and paused, her face a frosty mask.

"Mr. Chase."

"Sorry," said Zip, "I'm—well, one of the trainees asked me to stand in for him. To bring the prisoners their food."

He struggled to balance the tray in one hand as he rooted in his pocket with the other.

Sumner, eyes flat: "Which trainee." It was a statement, not a question.

"His name is James. He wanted to meet his mother for dinner," said Zip. He showed the pass card. The food almost tipped, and he lunged after it, barely regaining his balance.

"I see," said Sumner.

He lofted the tray. "Should I—"

"Go ahead."

He felt her eyes on his back as he passed. The cell

yawned before him. Inside, under the aquatic fluorescents, were cots, a toilet, and a desk. On one cot sat a woman with piercing eyes and hair tied up behind her head. On the other cot sprawled Lindsey Li.

Zip walked to the exact center of the room and knelt, prosthetic leg creaking, to set the tray on the floor. As he swiveled and rose, his gaze crossed Li's momentarily. She looked half dead in the pallid light, but her eyes were very much alive. Her hair was longer than he'd ever seen it. If she was surprised, she hid it completely.

Then he was out of the room, the door clanging shut behind him.

"Give me the pass card, please," said Sumner. His fingers brushed hers as he placed it in her hand. Her skin was unbelievably soft. She curled perfect unpainted nails around the card and left without a word.

Outside, he sat in the SUV and counted long, deep breaths. The parking lot gradually darkened. Blue lights flickered to life atop tall steel poles. When someone climbed into the car next to him, Zip shook himself and stuck the keys in the ignition.

Back at the hotel, he pounded furiously on Hollywood's door.

"No hablo room service," shouted Hollywood.

"It's me," said Zip, and pounded some more.

There was a commotion of rustling fabric and pattering feet. The door swung open to reveal a glowering Hollywood clad in nothing but clover-patterned boxer shorts.

"What?" he said.

"I found where they're keeping Li," said Zip.

"Congratulations," said Hollywood, thunking his head against the narrow edge of the door. "Let's talk about it in the morning."

A woman edged around the corner behind him, blanket held up to her neck. Naked skin glistened on either side. She said something sharp in Portuguese.

"Babe," said Hollywood, still thunking his head on the door, "you know I don't understand that shit."

His forehead had accrued a red rectangular mark.

"Who is the man?" asked the woman, eyes flashing like bug zappers.

Hollywood sighed.

"Alright," he muttered, "fine."

He pushed himself off the door and turned, revealing a musclebound back covered in scars.

"Git," he said, popping a thumb toward the door. "I'll call you tomorrow. Si?"

More Portuguese, very fast and close together. Hollywood squeezed the bridge of his misshapen nose. "Beat it, baby. Vamos. I'll buy you dinner, okay? Dinner?"

Rolling his eyes at Zip, he closed the door, cutting the torrent of invective in half. Zip observed his shoes until the door opened and she stormed past him, chin high, tugging a halter-top strap over her shoulder. She left a cloud of cloying perfume in her wake.

"I saw Li, Hollywood," said Zip as he lunged into the room. "She's alive."

"Unsurprising," said Hollywood. "She was always tougher than him."

"I know where she is," said Zip. "We can get them both out at once."

"Well," said Hollywood, "I had a productive day too."

Zip surveyed the graveyard of alcohol and street food. A fly circumnavigated a half-eaten döner kebab on the room's obligatory faded green armchair.

"Don't make that face," said Hollywood. "I found a guy who'll sell us guns."

"What kind?"

"Whatever we want. RPGs. Anti-personnel mines. Flamethrowers. He's a Russian dude. Eight feet tall, bald as an Egyptian cat, grizzly bear tattoo, three missing teeth... the works."

"So when are we doing it?"

"Fuck, man."

"Next week. Let's do it next week."

"We need more time."

"Two weeks after that, training will be wrapping up, they'll be trying to send you into the forest."

"We can't just— look, man, we need a *plan*."

Someone knocked insistently on the door.

"For the love of God," shouted Hollywood, stomping over and wrenching it open.

Hailey Sumner stood in the hallway, one eyebrow raised. Behind her loomed two hypervascular guards. Zip's lungs shriveled.

"You again," she said flatly.

"Um," said Zip.

"That's okay," said Sumner, flicking a hand at her craggy bodyguards, who took up positions in the hallway. "This concerns both of you."

"What does?" asked Hollywood.

"We need to move the schedule up," said Sumner. If it bothered her that Hollywood was clad only in boxers, she didn't show it.

"The trainees need more time," said Zip, thinking of James.

"They have the rest of the week," said Sumner, turning to Hollywood. "Sunday. Understood? And there's been a change of plans."

Hollywood ran a hand gingerly up the back of his neck. "Of course."

"The green one," said Sumner. "He's going with you."

Zip's jaw fell open. He snapped it shut.

"He'll still have the shock collar," said Sumner, "and we've figured out how to block his psychic link, so he can't call in reinforcements. But he's going to be your guide to the anomaly. Do you understand?"

"Yes ma'am," said Hollywood.

Sumner's eyes lingered on Zip.

"Wonderful," she said, and beamed. "You gentlemen have a pleasant evening, now."

The next morning, James didn't show up to training. He wasn't there the day after that, either. When Zip asked the others about him, they avoided his eyes. Eventually he stopped asking.

21

As they made their way into the forest, Hollywood studied the eccentricities of his Omphalos companions. The biggest, meanest one, who by virtue of his bigness and meanness seemed to be the leader, had a name like Klaus or Krauss. He carried one of the devices that activated Tetris's shock collar. Klaus or possibly Krauss had demonstrated this capability early on the first day, when Tetris failed to rise from his lunch break with sufficient alacrity. A judicious button press on Klaus/Krauss's transmitter had sent the green ranger convulsing to his knees.

Three of the seven soldiers had mustaches. All seven

had at least one visible tattoo, several of which depicted snakes intertwined. One of the mustached men had scales tattooed on his neck. A heavyset man everybody called Dondo carried a preposterous six-barreled minigun, with ribbons of ammo draped all over him, but he didn't seem to notice the weight. Dondo had, in addition to the bushy hair on his upper lip, a full-bodied red beard tied in little knots. He'd cut off the sleeves of his uniform, revealing enormous biceps, upon the right of which an anatomically precise tattoo of a human heart throbbed as he walked.

One of the more modestly-tattooed individuals was a skittish, swarthy man who could have appeared, smiling confidently, on a package of boxer briefs. His dark hair maintained its pointy front edge no matter the humidity. Hollywood woke one morning to find him hard at work with a comb and travel mirror.

The soldiers took turns leading Tetris by the chain attached to his collar. His hands remained shackled at all times. At night, they affixed the chain to the branch and kept watch in shifts. The close surveillance prevented Hollywood from getting in range, until one afternoon the soldier on duty asked him to hold the chain while he stepped around a tree for a piss.

"Surprise," hissed Hollywood, examining Tetris's shock collar. It was disconcerting to have to look up at him. One of his pinkies was missing, and his arms were criss-crossed with gnarly scars. Across the clearing, Klaus/Krauss eyed them suspiciously.

"I've known for weeks," said Tetris.

The soldier returned before he could explain any further. Hollywood handed the chain over and stepped away, picking at grime on his SCAR-17.

Though he never would have admitted it, Hollywood didn't have a plan. Even if they overpowered the soldiers, there was no way to unlock the collar, which contained a tracker. Leaving the collar intact was hardly an option if they wanted to avoid a warm welcome on shore. The problem seemed unsolvable. He'd think of something, though. He always did.

On a normal expedition, Hollywood and Zip would have argued vehemently against loading up with ponderous firepower, but in this case they hadn't bothered. As a result, the group that ventured into the forest was larger, louder, and better-armed than any Hollywood had ever seen. A man named Andri had an AK-47 and three sidearms strapped to his body—one on each hip, plus an enormous revolver holstered under his left arm. Another man had an antitank rocket launcher, with an ammo case over his shoulder that kept slipping off. Rocket launcher guy, spooked, fired into a hollow log on the second day. Centipedes came wriggling out while Hollywood armed his grapple gun and grimly ascended.

Soldiers trying to operate grapple guns while carrying rocket launchers and miniguns, not to mention ammunition, were a thing of comic beauty. Half the time they couldn't figure out how to clamber onto the branches they'd hooked, so they dangled underneath like lopsided fruit until it was time to descend. Andri fumbled his AK-

47 during one ascent and had to root in the undergrowth afterward. Along the way he brushed a plant that gave him a ferocious rash.

On the third night, Hollywood had a dream. An unshackled Tetris with dead eyes led him around a skyscraper-sized tree, pausing on the other side to point out a stand of orange flowers. Hollywood looked at the flowers. He looked at dream-Tetris, who pointed again at the flowers. Hollywood looked back at the flowers. Then he woke up.

When they stopped for lunch the next day, and Hollywood took a few steps out of the clearing to relieve himself, he found a stand of ... orange flowers. Normally he would have left anything that colorful alone, but he was so astounded by the coincidence that he reached out to brush one of the petals.

Just before his fingers made contact, a bee buzzed in and landed on the nest of protuberances in the center. A thread of smoke rose immediately. With a soft hiss, the insect melted, dripping into the depths until only a slight odor of burnt plastic remained.

Hollywood retracted his hand. Gingerly, with a twig, he prodded the flower on all sides. When he pressed the tip against the petals, it released a tiny wisp of chemical smoke. But the flower's green underside was harmless. Hollywood dropped the smoldering twig and wiped his sweaty hands on his pants. The plant's leaves were wide and shiny. He tore one off and touched it to the blossom. Sure enough, the leaf was unharmed. He ripped off several more and carefully wrapped a flower, then folded the package up in yet more leaves and tucked it in the side of his pack.

That night, as he tried to fall asleep, he heard Tetris talking to the soldier on watch.

"Nocturnal predators hunt by heat," said Tetris.

"Shut up," said the soldier.

"There could be a blood bat zeroing in right now. You wouldn't know until it grabbed you."

Hollywood heard the slight buzz and accompanying grunt that indicated a low-grade jolt from the shock collar.

"That wasn't very nice," said Tetris.

"Shut up," said the soldier again, in the slightly muffled way of a person who has his molars clenched together.

Tetris chuckled. It was a deep sound, minatory, and Hollywood swallowed despite himself. Green Tetris reminded him of a caged and brutalized pit bull.

Before they set out the next morning, Klaus/Krauss took hold of Hollywood's jacket.

"It just occurred to me," he growled, "that you were a ranger."

The others stopped to watch. Tetris stared into the green distance, still as a stone idol.

"Just now? It's alright. We can't all be Stephen Hawking-grade intellects," said Hollywood.

"Careful with this mouth of yours."

"I suppose you thought I landed the job with a strongly worded cover letter."

"He was a ranger too."

215

"So I've heard."

"You wouldn't have happened to run across him, I hope. In your previous life."

"There are lots of rangers. What was your name, again?"

The soldier stuck a finger in his ear and twisted, then examined the accumulation of orange wax. "My name is Felix Krauss."

"Klaus? Like as in 'Santa Claus?'"

"Like as in, there is an 'R,' not an 'L.'"

"Krauss. Thanks for clearing that up."

"Stay away from the prisoner."

"Fine by me. He's got a bit of an aroma. Y'all ever let him shower?"

"You are expendable," said Krauss. "If it becomes necessary, I will expend you."

"Taking some liberties with my native language, there, but I get your drift."

"I will spoon your eyeballs from your skull. With a spoon. Does that make for an understanding?"

"Loud and clear, boss. No spoonerisms necessary."

Three hours later, they came across a Megadodo. The harmless giant came stumbling out of the vegetation and, upon seeing them, produced an extremely loud noise. The nuances of the noise—terror, surprise, and general brainlessness—were lost on the soldiers, whose basic impression of the situation was that a three-story bird intended to eat them.

Dondo unleashed the minigun. Andri emptied his AK-

47. Rocket launcher guy fired his rocket launcher and missed, taking a big chunk out of an innocent tree. The Megadodo ran away, as it had intended to do anyway. Taking advantage of the general disarray, a trapdoor spider burst from its burrow, snatched a soldier, and dragged him kicking and screaming into its tunnel.

The others ran over and poured an otiose flood of lead into the burrow. Grenades were hurled, detonating with great subterranean thunks. Hollywood washed his hands of the situation and grapple-gunned away. Tetris stood grinning at the soldier who held his leash, who trembled like a newborn giraffe, finger hovering over the shock transmitter's big red button.

A few days earlier, the rocket launcher's discharge into a hollow log had gone more or less unnoticed, perhaps because the single loud crash approximated the sound of a falling tree. The amount of firepower discharged at and around the Megadodo, and subsequently into the trapdoor spider's burrow, could not be attributed to natural forces. It was probably the most aurally stimulating occurrence in this part of the forest's recent memory, and it provoked a correspondingly enthusiastic response.

A scorpion skidded out of the vegetation, shrugged off blistering fire, and speared the handsome swarthy soldier with its stinger. A pterodactyl dove past Hollywood on titanic leathery wings, only to be tackled out of the air by a creature with a body like a frog and a huge, circular mouth where its face was supposed to be. The buzzsawmouthed frog-thing had leapt some forty feet into the air to catch its prey, and the two creatures fell in a complex bloody tumble into a copse of thornbushes, while from the opposite direction a six-legged lizard came tail-lashing into the clearing. The soldiers dispersed as the lizard darted between them, flinching under the blunt percussive force of Dondo's minigun.

Standing amid the chaos, Tetris smiled. His teeth shone white as naked bone. He turned to the soldier with his chain, who was enthralled by a tarantula clambering delicately down a nearby tree. When the soldier began to back away, Tetris stuck out a foot and tripped him. The soldier slammed a hand on the transmitter's button as he fell, and Tetris crumpled. The tarantula paused, feeling the air with two enormous legs, a few yards away. The lizard had gotten hold of Andri and stood chewing him contemplatively as the others bellowed and unloaded their worthless weapons.

Convulsing, Tetris crawled toward the man with the transmitter as fire directed at both the lizard and the tarantula whizzed over his head. The clearing crackled with gunfire, shouts, and the screeches of approaching wildlife. The soldier with the transmitter scrabbled and kicked, trying to keep away from Tetris. Not fast enough. Tetris grasped a foot and yanked him closer. The man let go of the device and took up his rifle. Tetris, hands still shackled, pushed the barrel away. Bullets sprayed up in a deadly arc. On a branch high above, Hollywood ducked. When he peered down again, the rifle had been tossed aside. Tetris wrestled the transmitter out of the man's hand and turned it off. He dragged the man to his feet, oblivious to the tracers filling the air, and hurled him at the tarantula. Fangs slipped effortlessly through the man's back and out his front as the horrible legs folded him up and brought him under the mouth to feed.

Tetris didn't bother watching. Hands still cuffed, he stalked toward Krauss, who had the key to the handcuffs in a loop at his waist. The unfolding madness might has well have been a hologram for all the attention he paid it. As the lizard that had just finished Andri turned with interest to a Dondo frantically loading another ribbon into his smoking minigun, Krauss dropped his empty rifle and fled. Tetris sprinted after him. On the far side of a tree, Krauss stopped, transmitter in one hand and a pistol in the other. He hit the button just as Tetris rounded the corner. The hulking ranger fell. Krauss leaned down and pressed the pistol against Tetris's broad green forehead.

Hollywood removed the top of Krauss's skull with a staccato burst from his SCAR-17.

"Stick a spoon in that, bitch," he shouted.

Tetris, drenched in blood and brain matter, shoved the corpse away and grasped the transmitter with spasming fingers. He turned it off, ripped the keys from Krauss's belt, contorted to unlock his cuffs, and, thusly freed, rolled onto his back with arms splayed wide. He closed his eyes. Bullets ripped overhead. A giant rat snuffled past him, took hold of the half-headless corpse, and tugged it through a hole in the ground.

Ten seconds passed. Hollywood didn't dare leave his tree. The action had moved elsewhere, out of sight, though the sound of gunfire had not abated. Finally Tetris climbed to his feet, armed his grapple gun, and joined Hollywood on the branch.

"Get my collar off," said Tetris.

"What?" said Hollywood.

"The flower," said Tetris. "Use it on the collar."

Hollywood rummaged in his pack and retrieved the leaf-wrapped orange blossom. The air convulsed with screeches and screams. Gingerly, holding the base in a shiny leaf, Hollywood pressed the petals against the collar. The air filled with the smell of burning copper. Foul black smoke rose in twisting columns. Hollywood held his breath. His eyes watered and stung. After a few seconds, he took the flower away.

Tetris grasped the collar with both hands. As it continued to smoke, the metal visibly blistering, he tensed his arms and wrenched once, hard. The collar split open. He removed it from his neck, wincing as a tiny streak of corrosive substance ate into his skin, and flung the heavy ring into empty space.

No sooner had Tetris's arm completed the motion of the throw than he buckled and nearly fell off the branch. His eyes rolled up in his head, and his mouth worked soundlessly. A dull roar built from the depths of his throat. The roar increased in volume until it became clear that it wasn't just coming from him. The trees flexed and whipped as if struck by hurricane winds. Hollywood slammed a climbing pick into the branch and held Tetris tight. Out of the canopy poured black-winged dragons. The forest floor shuddered and caved as a legion of subway snakes roiled to the surface. Hollywood pressed his cheek against the bark and held his breath. He wished his hands were free so he could stick fingers in his ears. Far below, a minigunless Dondo attempted to navigate the tremoring ground and fell, windmilling, into the maw of a snake.

Tetris roared anew. Like a reanimated corpse, he jerked around to stare at Hollywood.

His pupils were black pits. Worms wriggled in the whites of his eyes.

Hollywood let him go and grasped the climbing pick with both hands. Tetris grapple-gunned away. A tornado of dragons swirled after him. The air itself leapt and sang. Great heaving snakes tore the ground to shreds as they went, revealing bottomless chasms and skeletons of trees long dead, the whole subterranean hellscape teeming with spiders, while behind it all, Hollywood closed his eyes and prayed to every god he'd ever heard of for the cataclysm to end.

22

Later the video would be replayed one billion times, broken down frame by frame and pixel by pixel. Total clarity was impossible. The camera responsible for the footage, which was mounted on a Portuguese Coast Guard tower, had the resolution of a department store security feed.

The black and white video opened with the forest at night, spotlights lapping at the treeline, the canopy rippling gently in the cool winter breeze. A human figure emerged. His arms were long, with big hands swinging at the ends, and his walk was purposeful. For a few moments the footage went on like that, the man stalking alone across the frame as the forest swayed ever-so-slightly behind him. Then spiders began to pour out of the trees. Thousands of legs flashed, the creatures carrying themselves low to the ground, hurrying as though pained by the stark pools of light. There was no end to them.

Next came enormous snakes. The spiders gave them a wide berth, scuttling to keep the rumbling paths clear. Huge shapes burst from the canopy and cut rapidly across the view. Freeze frames would reveal these creatures to be tremendous reptiles with clustered black eyes and mouths packed with so many slender teeth that they seemed to be perpetually smiling.

The flood continued until a snake bumped against the base of the concrete tower. For a moment the camera caught a view of the ground below, a landscape of tangled arachnids and torrential, scaly flesh, and then, after a few frames of plummet, the feed cut out.

*****

Tetris's army had barely crossed the perimeter when the Portuguese military met them head-on. The horde produced a chittering roar, laced by steel-on-glass screams from the dragons that swirled overhead, but even that couldn't mask the shuddering cry of jet fighters puncturing the troposphere.

When the first air-to-ground missiles struck, all sound ceased, orange plumes leaping up to Tetris's right and left, spider parts flying, a gutted subway snake rising near-vertically out of the flames. The heat seared Tetris's neck—and as suddenly as the sounds had cut out, they came rushing back. The force of the nearest explosion knocked him off his feet as his army burst in all directions.

Ahead, white light erupted from a dozen apertures. There came a whistling sensation and the belated retort of tanks firing, while dirt rose spattering and crescents of shrapnel hummed overhead.

He stumbled onward, surrounded by spiders. A dragon fell out of the sky and wrenched a tank barrel upward just as it fired. The backblast sent tank and dragon up in a candent yellow-white pillar. Other dragons fell upon soldiers huddled behind makeshift barriers. Chuckling gunfire did little to dissuade their fearsome claws and teeth.

Tetris ran. A subway snake bulled down a line, bucking tanks like toy cars. Treads spun worthlessly against smoky dark space. The creature's mouth worked relentlessly, half distended, snapping up soldiers and equipment and earth. Spiders threw themselves into the barriers and fell twitching under withering fire, only to be replaced by more and more and more, an endless wriggling curtain. Another tank detonated as Tetris slid into a crater.

KILLKILLKILLKILLKILLKILL, said the forest.

A soldier rose out of the darkness with a rifle and Tetris ducked. He catapulted underneath screaming orange tracers, slammed against the soldier and rolled, hands working on their own to find the vulnerable skull and twist. Vertebrae popped. The hunger glowed all the stronger. Some part of him reeled, trying to vomit, but that part was not in control.

He didn't look at the dead soldier's face, just picked himself up and kept going. The air smelled of sulfur and blood. Immense wreaths of gunsmoke clouded his night vision. Into the fog he plunged, trusting the windmilling legs all around him, following the cries and clicks of a swarm in which he was just another hungry mouth.

By the time he reached Omphalos headquarters, air raid sirens blared from the center of Lisbon. The forest buzzed in his skull. He aimed his grapple gun at a window and fired, but the silver spearhead bounced right off. He tried the door. Spiders milled in the parking lot. Several clustered around a car, probing it with hooked feet. Tetris approached.

"Back," he shouted, projecting the command with telepathic force. The spiders retreated.

Inside cowered a fat man with enormous fleshy ears, wearing the green and black uniform of the Omphalos Initiative. Tetris knocked on the glass. The man didn't respond. Tetris smashed the window with his elbow. Glass rained everywhere. His boot soles crunched as he reached inside and flicked the lock. He opened the door and dragged the man out.

KILLKILLKILLKILLKILLKILL

"Tell me where the prisoners are," said Tetris.

"B3," said the man. "11 and 14. Oh God, please!"

"Badge," said Tetris.

The man clawed at the green hand constricting his neck.

"*Badge,*" said Tetris.

The man rooted in his pocket and produced the access badge. Tetris snatched it, but his other hand refused to release.

KILLKILLKILLKILLKILLKILL

He grit his teeth and fought the forest. Sweat droplets burst across his forehead.

KILLKILLKILLKILLKILLKILL

Spiders closed in, caressing the man with their forelegs, chittering in Tetris's ear. The man screamed high and long. Tetris expelled air, fighting the command, veins bulging along his neck. With a final cry, he tore his hand away. The spiders recoiled. The forest's voice retreated to a distant throb.

"Go," Tetris panted. "Go!"

The man sobbed, climbed into his car, and swerved away.

Tetris staggered to the door, scanned the badge, and stood back as he pulled it open, expecting a flood of lead. Nothing happened. He peered around the edge. It was dark as the far side of Jupiter, though that didn't matter to him anymore. The hallway was empty. He strode inside and the spiders flowed after him, a complex black-carapaced tapestry.

The elevator was locked. Tetris cracked his knuckles and squeezed his fingers into the gap between the doors. Strained. Took a deep breath and pulled, to no avail. The spiders joined him, braced against the opposite wall and each other. They chattered and hissed, pulling. The doors groaned. Slowly, laboriously, they began to slide open. Cold air rushed out of the shaft.

Tetris leaned in and hooked his grapple gun around a

metal outcropping. As he rappelled, the spiders followed, working their way down the wall. The shaft filled with their clicking speech.

Three floors down, Tetris kicked the override switch on the wall, and the doors sprang open.

He rolled into the hall, inches beneath a blistering wall of fire. If the spiders hadn't burst out after him, catching the bullets with their armored exoskeletons, he would have been perforated like a cheese grater. When the last of the spiders had passed, and the gunshots had been replaced by the patter of six thousand chitinous feet, Tetris rose and followed.

He passed a mangled pile of corpses at the T-intersection just as a soldier groggily rolled a green and black-uniformed body aside and raised a tremulous pistol. Tetris snatched the pistol, stuck it in his belt, and lifted the man to his feet.

"Where's B3-11?" he demanded. "Where are the prisoners?"

The soldier mouthed silently. Blood flowed freely from a gash in his neck.

"Flown away," he choked. His eyes rolled up in his head.

Tetris dropped him and pressed onward. He found two empty cells, 11 and 14. He pounded a four-fingered fist into his palm until the stub of his pinky finger screamed. Where?

He sprinted back to the elevator. Outside, the clouds had cleared, revealing a moon like an cross-section of broken femur. Tetris stood in the empty parking lot and allowed his body to quake. The southwest horizon glowed orange-purple, flames scrabbling against the star-flecked sky. Distant cries and roars intermixed with jet engine skirls and thumping artillery fire. Tetris extended his arms and called the chaos to him, vibrating, beaming messages at a forest whose attention was divided among a million skittering fingers.

As the cries of dragons grew louder, an SUV careened around the corner. Tetris drew the pistol from his belt and approached. The passenger-side window rolled down.

"Get in," shouted Zip, leaning over to shove the door open.

Stunned, Tetris climbed inside.

"I figured you'd come here," said Zip.

"Li and Doc," said Tetris.

"Gone?"

Tetris closed his eyes. *Where?*

He tapped the gold strand linking him to the forest. Images flicker-flashed: a subway snake bursting into an artillery encampment and knocking the great gun on its side. A dragon carrying a soldier to the red roof of a building before shredding the gooey meal through meat-grinder teeth.

Flown away.

"The airport," said Tetris.

Zip spun the wheel and floored it. They roared down desolate boulevards as flames glowed and trembled in the rear-view mirror. Spiders poured out of the shadows and galloped after them. Dragons whirled and beat their wings above.

As they neared the airport, Tetris received another image-flash. Three figures in shackles, accompanied by a mob of soldiers, a single tall figure at the front of the pack, all of them walking the long distance to a private jet marooned on the tarmac. The engines were spinning up.

"They're on the runway," said Tetris.

Zip wrenched the SUV off the main road and toward a series of abandoned guard towers. Fences rose like silver webs on either side, tipped with bundled barbed wire. They smashed through the yellow-black arms of a security checkpoint and onto the tarmac.

Tetris beamed his need at the forest. Another blast of images: this time a sunny place, China, defoliants dropped by the ton on the coastal canopy. The screaming psychic pain of innumerable neurons shriveling.

KILLKILLKILLKILLKILLKILL

"Stop the plane," Tetris thought/said.

A dragon fell out of the sky and struck the private jet, knocking it down the runway with big holes in the fuselage. An engine slurped up the tip of the dragon's lashing tail. As the beast screamed and spun and tried to pull away, black blood spitting out the back of the turbine, the whole wing went up in a ball of flame. Then the swarm arrived, with Zip and Tetris at its ravenous head.

When Tetris saw the burn scars on the man at the front of the line, an animal hatred consumed him. As Zip hit the handbrake and swung the vehicle around, Tetris kicked the door open and flung himself out. He tumbled across the pavement, rolled roughly on his shoulder, and righted himself. Canines bared, he lunged for the scar-faced man.

Taking advantage of the commotion, Li struck the nearest guard with two hands. She wrapped her cuffs around his neck, spun, and kicked another guard in the chin. Vincent and Dr. Alvarez struggled with their own assailants. Then the spiders arrived. Gunfire snapped as Tetris pounded a fist into the scarred man's jaw again and again.

Soldiers fled down the runway, spiders in pursuit. As Li and the others un-clicked their handcuffs, Tetris lifted the burn-faced man's hand and bit off two of his fingers.

KILLKILLKILLKILLKILLKILL, said the forest.

The burn-faced man screamed. Tetris tasted salty-sweet blood and spit the fingers away. He dropped the hand, grabbed the man's hair, and slammed his skull down. The man kept screaming. Blood fountained from his finger stumps. Li and Dr. Alvarez froze just shy of intervening while Vincent staggered up behind them, clutching his shoulder.

Tetris cradled the man's head with two enormous green thumbs poised half an inch over the eyeballs.

"Don't do it," said Li.

The man lay frozen and silent, staring at the thumbs occupying his entire field of view.

The forest thrummed and roared in Tetris's skull. He imagined plunging his thumbs into the eyeballs, then through into the brain, the wonderful squelching give. He wanted it so bad. The blood in his mouth hummed and sang. He was a cosmic force, one with the universe.

"It's unnecessary," said Li.

The scarred man stared at the thumbs. Tetris fought, panting. How many times had cigarettes been pressed against his skin? How many fingernails and toenails had been ripped off, only to see them grow back again? How many times had the car battery been wheeled into the room? Tetris closed his eyes and caressed the eyelids. So fragile. So easy. The ease of it called to him. Easy as the scarred man's meat cleaver separating a green pinky from its shivering hand. Press quickly and hard, ignore the thrashing, ignore the blood. Catharsis. He knew he didn't have to. He knew, on some level, that it would be wrong. But he wanted it so bad.

His fingers twitched. Across the tarmac, the flaming jet crackled quietly. A breeze swept across the airfield, heavy with the scent of ash and death.

KILL, said the forest.

Tetris released the torturer's head, struck him hard under the jaw to knock him out, and stood.

"Not today," he mumbled, and tottered toward the SUV.

23

"Where's your finger, T?"

Tetris glanced at his hands on the wheel. No left pinky.

"They wanted to see if it would grow back," he said.

"It did not."

"No, it did not."

The others were asleep in the back seat. Li had her window open and a hand in the shape of a wing swooping up and down in the wind.

"I killed a lot of people," said Tetris.

"Don't think about it."

"I want to think about it, but I can't."

"Good."

"The only thing I can think about, after months of the shit they fed us, is how bad I want a milkshake."

"Do they have those here?"

"They've gotta have fast food chains, right?"

"Presumably."

He turn-signaled into an exit lane.

"Which flavor would you want?" asked Li.

"Chocolate. No. Strawberry."

"A place near me had peach milkshakes during the summer. Simply incredible."

"I snapped a guy's neck, Li."

"Mint chocolate chip. Now that's tried and true."

"Some soldier. I felt his spine snap. Like twisting a plastic tower until the pieces went flying. Blood shot out of his mouth."

"You did what you had to do."

"I had a choice. I think I wanted to kill him."

Li watched scattered buildings flicker by. "What's the plan, here? This is a hamlet. They don't have chain restaurants. They might not even have plumbing."

Tetris kept driving, out the far side of the town and into the empty countryside. Farmland unfurled between meandering hedges. The sound of the wind through Li's open window was a flexing, snapping roar. She put a knife in her hair and sawed.

"I think I enjoyed it, is the thing," said Tetris. "I think I enjoy killing people."

"Tetris, shut the fuck up."

For a long time, nobody said anything. They stopped for gas around six in the morning. Li disembarked to handle it. When Tetris checked on the others, Zip was grinning at him. Dr. Alvarez lay asleep on his shoulder.

"You crazy motherfuckers," said Zip. "You're alive. You're actually alive."

It had been a rough couple of months for the forest. First its only conduit and link to the human world had vanished. Then China began covertly testing defoliants on the canopy off their coast. Through the world's radio transmissions, the forest heard itself endlessly vilified. Extremist politicians everywhere took advantage of forest-fear to win elections against odds that had previously seemed insurmountable. Still reeling from the nuclear strike on one of its neurological centers, the forest began to lose intermittent control of its extremities. Trees along the borders with the polar wastes shriveled and fell. A section of forest off the Western European coast went fuzzy and faded in and out.

With no response to its exhaustive psychic probings, the forest came to the logical conclusion: Tetris had been imprisoned, experimented upon, and dissected by the Portuguese government. After all, it was the police who'd turned him over. Seething over the abduction and murder of its sole ambassador, the forest plotted retribution.

Roots trapped spider queens and subway snakes, holding them close and venting anesthetic clouds so that the forest's pseudopods could conduct the surgeries and genetic engineering necessary to bring their electromagnetic receptors in line. Dragons served for reconnaissance and aerial intimidation, while subway snakes provided raw armored force, and spiders filled the gaps. An army of fangs and claws and mountainous muscle began to coalesce.

A week before Tetris's reappearance, the Chinese went public with plans to defoliate a thirty-mile buffer along their entire coast. The staggering expense didn't dissuade them, although it did enrage a certain world-spanning entity that would much rather have seen those funds invested in planetary defense. Plus the defoliation hurt. Every tree in the forest was essentially a neuron. A certain amount of attrition was to be expected, and the psychic structure of the forest adjusted constantly to compensate, but full-scale deforestation cascaded static across the entire network.

*****

"We go now to the US Embassy in Portugal for an exclusive interview with American private security contractor Jehovah Donahue, a former Army captain who participated in yesterday's frantic eleventh-hour defense. Jehovah: how's it going over there?"

"It's a real clusterfu—a real bad situation, Kathy."

"We've all seen the reports. An unprecedented terrestrial incursion by the forest. Thousands of casualties. What I want to know is, how did it feel on the ground?"

"Well, Kathy, there's no surrendering to a giant snake.

And the flying fu—ahem, *creatures*—I saw one rip a man in half and eat both halves. Grisly stuff. Blood everywhere. Theirs and ours. Whole rivers of blood. The ground just muddy with it. The air like whumping and cracking with wingbeats. I was in the Army for ten years, Kathy. I served in Afghanistan. Nothing prepared me for this."

"In the wake of this disaster, do you think training regimens will have to adapt?"

"Oh, absolutely. I mean, it's a war, right? It's our enemy. So we'll obviously have to learn to fight it better."

"I understand that your defense in Lisbon was successful, though, in the sense that it drove back the invaders?"

"Yes."

"So you won."

"I mean, 'won' kind of fails to capture the on-the-ground reality, if I'm honest, ma'am. More like the other side decided to leave."

"Why Portugal, do you think? Why attack there, of all places?"

"If you ask me, it's a message. The forest wants to scare us. My biggest worry is that our current administration isn't up to the challenge."

"You don't think the President is tough enough on the forest?"

"With all due respect, ma'am, I do not. He's a nice guy. I'd love to grab a beer with him. But when it comes to leading the free world against the greatest threat humanity's ever faced—I don't think he's qualified."

*****

"If our link was blocked, how did you send me those dreams?"

What dreams?

"About the orange flowers that could eat through my collar."

Silence.

"Hello?"

I didn't send any dreams.

"How is that possible?"

But the forest was gone again.

They were holed up in a barn in the Spanish countryside. Dr. Alvarez had negotiated with the owner for a one-week stay. The barn smelled of manure and horse sweat. Hay bales served as beds. Tetris paced, peeking through cloudy windows into the flat black night. Somewhere out there, Hollywood was headed toward them. When he reached the coast he'd give Zip a call on the burner they'd prepared for this purpose.

Everyone was asleep. Tetris couldn't stand the stillness, so he slipped out the door.

Moisture beaded on his skin. He wished for a jacket. A big moon hung just overhead, backed by a spray of white-blue stars. The Milky Way smeared across the sky. Trees that formed the edge of the farmer's property stooped in the breeze. Whenever he closed his eyes, he saw the Portuguese soldier's shadowed face, or the gruesome amphitheater of Krauss's ruptured skull.

Crickets creaked. An animal rooted in the undergrowth. Tetris lay down in the wet grass and rubbed his eyes with the heel of his hand. It was dangerous to be out here. The farmer hadn't seen him yet, and would surely inform the authorities if he did. But the grass felt good.

After a while he climbed a tree.

When the sun finally rose, he slipped back into the barn and prepared breakfast, SPAM and eggs sizzling on a propane stove.

"Chef Tetris on the case," said Zip, who came hopping over, affixing his prosthetic, when he smelled the food.

"Old family recipe," said Tetris.

He held the pancake mix in one hand, trying to decipher the instructions, while he flipped eggs with the other.

"I missed you, buddy," said Zip.

"You too," said Tetris. He put the spatula down and rooted in the cooler for a milk carton.

"I didn't take you for a cook," said Dr. Alvarez. She sat beside Zip on the long oak bench.

"Prepare for pancakes that will blow your mind."

He poured the mixture into a bowl, added milk, and stirred. Li stretched near the door, touching her nose to her knee.

"Your eggs are burning," she called as she switched to the other leg.

He almost dropped the batter bowl. "Shit. Shit!"

"Yeah," said Zip, giving the scraped-up eggs a dubious look, "those ones are yours, big guy."

The pancakes were done by the time Vincent made it over. The agent took a plate without comment and retreated to his corner.

"What's wrong with him?" asked Zip.

Tetris wiped his hands on a rag.

"He's just sulking," said Li. "You'll get used to it."

After breakfast Li and Dr. Alvarez climbed into the loft. Vincent sat in the corner, massaging his shoulder and doodling on a pad of warped yellow paper.

"I didn't know you could draw," said Tetris when he walked by to dump the trash out. A jungle landscape sprawled across Vincent's notepad, populated by spiders and snakes. The lines were confident and strong.

"It's nothing," said Vincent. He tore the page off and wadded it up.

"Man," said Tetris, catching the crumpled ball en route to the trash can, "that's really amazing."

Vincent rubbed his shoulder. Tetris unfolded the drawing.

"You hurt?" he asked, trying to smooth the creases.

"I'm fine," said Vincent.

"You keep touching your shoulder."

"Old injury."

"What happened?"

"Gunshot."

Tetris peered at him. "Gunshot."

"I was a cop," said Vincent.

"I could believe that."

The agent picked at skin around his fingernails.

"You're the kind of guy who only believes in black and white," said Tetris. "Right and wrong."

"No."

"That's why you don't like me. No patience for the chaotic neutral."

"Reason I don't like you is you're an asshole."

"You were an only child, I suspect."

"I had two brothers."

"Well. I bet you got along real well with them, huh?"

Vincent didn't reply. He rotated the pencil stub back and forth.

*****

The days dragged on, each more monotonous than the last. Sometimes the farmer came to visit, forcing Tetris to hide in the loft, wedged beneath the sloped ceiling, until Li gave him the all-clear. He wasn't the only one feeling cooped up. When the food ran out, everyone was so eager to get off the farm that they went to town and left Tetris behind. He prowled and paced and counted knots in the bare plank walls. Somehow he'd expected that escaping the cell would mean an end to inaction. Instead he was back to doing nothing, dribbling time through his fingers like mud, unsure whether he wanted it to flow slower or faster.

If the days were purgatory, the nights were far worse.

Eight hours of uninterrupted silence, without even the forest to keep him company most of the time. He got so bored that he began to pray for something to happen. Anything at all.

One lonesome nocturnal vigil, he spotted a pair of hunched shapes making their way across the night-glassed lawn. The way they moved, furtive and scuttling, you could tell they were up to no good. Burglars? Murderers? Tetris closed his eyes and reached out the way he'd learned to do in the Omphalos cell. The trespassers' auras tasted like melted plastic. Emitting acrid psychic fumes, they drifted towards the farmhouse.

Tetris opened his eyes just in time to see knives come twinkling out of sheaths as the figures stepped onto the farmer's porch. One man's shoulder brushed a wind chime. In the motionless air, the tinkling sounded somehow profane.

Tetris went to the back door of the barn and slid it quietly open.

His night vision didn't make things brighter—it was dark as a walled-off mine shaft—but he could see nonetheless. Every edge of grass stood out in calcified relief. Only a portion of the image was visual. According to the forest, Tetris's custom-built night vision pooled echolocation and electromagnetic spectra on the fringes of visible light, the clamoring sensory potpourri relayed down sparking nerve networks to a newly swollen region of his brain, where overtime neural efforts produced a composite image more reminiscent of an etching in obsidian than a photograph.

Point being that his days of stumbling after rabbits were over. This was Tetris Aphelion v1.3, a far cry from Vanilla T, with more patches undoubtedly on the way. Night vision had come fully online during their march through the Atlantic. When he'd descended into the chasm with Toni Davis in his arms, Tetris had been able to see the tendrils gather her in. The look on her unconscious face, he remembered, had been peaceful, her mouth hanging open as the leg wound suppurated through its wrappings...

He stalked across the open ground, quiet and ominous as an upper-canopy breeze.

The robbers had left the door swinging gently on its hinges. Tetris traced a finger along the wood as he passed. He rode the liquid darkness that rushed ahead to lap against peeling wallpaper and framed family photos. Red-rimmed auras led him up the stairs and down the hall to the master bedroom.

Lights snapped on, casting huge knife-wielding shadows into the hallway. A voice cried out. Tetris stood a few yards back, the balls of his bare feet kissing the hardwood, and took a deep breath through his nose.

The trespasser on the left was thickset and bald, with a purple splotch the shape of France on his shiny skull. On the right slouched a man as hirsute as the first burglar was hairless. Black curls protruded from the collar of his worn blue polo.

On the far side of the room, shielded by a massive four-poster bed, the farmer held a WWII-era rifle, its ancient barrel vacillating from target to target.

The bald trespasser said something in Spanish and gestured with his knife.

The farmer's gun froze. He stared at Tetris, who loomed above and behind the thugs, head just shy of the doorframe.

Spitting, the hirsute trespasser said something that sounded like a curse. He took a step forward. The bald one took a step in the opposite direction, pincering around the bed.

Tetris stepped in, palmed the skull of the bald trespasser, and flung him face-first into the wall. He enjoyed the movement, the simple casual flick, the deep shuddering boom when face met siding. Enjoyed the quick pivot and reach for the second man, whose spinning face broadcast the abject terror of a horror movie jump-scare. For the thug, the darkness had parted to reveal six and a half feet of huge-pupiled boogeyman. Before the would-be robber's brain could begin to parse the impending fight/flight dilemma, Tetris's knee planted itself midway up his chest.

The whole process took no more than two seconds: Tetris appearing, one quick step, first trespasser flung, a pivot so swift that splayed toes squeaked on wood, then one more step and a falcon-like strike with the non-stepping knee. The kneed, hairy thug approached the wall with velocity that suggested, like, two hundred percent, easy. The sound was BOOM-squeak-BOOM, followed by the double-whump of bodies hitting the floor milliseconds apart.

"You're okay," said Tetris, raising a calming hand to the farmer and his wife.

The farmer pointed the antique firearm at Tetris's head and pulled the trigger. Nothing happened.

"Jesus, man," said Tetris, coming up from a duck. "What's wrong with you?"

The thug who'd received the knee lunged along the floor with his serrated knife Achilles-bound. Tetris leapt the strike and landed stumbling on the man's back while the other thug came staggering over, knife wavering, nose not so much broken as forcibly retracted into his face.

On the other side of the bed, the farmer frantically worked at unjamming his weapon, a detail Tetris noted with some trepidation while he tried to figure out how to avoid the two crazily-slashing knives. A blade bit his arm and he roared, right hand dribbling the prone assailant's face against the hardwood while his free hand reached and grabbed what turned out to be the crotch of the upright slashing bloody-faced bald guy. Then, with some kind of off-kilter drunken surge, Tetris rose, applying his shoulder liberally to the chest of the man whose you-know-whats were clutched so unpleasantly in his huge green hand. A flip and a shove and the bald man returned to the wall he'd hit originally, upside down and with considerably more force, actually rupturing the drywall this time, and then a shot rang out, as the farmer at last convinced his weapon to fire.

Despite squirming slabs of muscle occupying sixty to seventy percent of his field of view, the farmer missed everything. The 50s-era heirloom bullet screamed across the hall into the bathroom, where it busted a pipe. As water shrieked through the gap, Tetris hunched and hobbled around the face-down home invader's blind desperate knife swings, finally dropping a fist on the back of the shaggy head. The knife arm went boneless.

Another shot, this one tickling his hair—

Out Tetris went, into the hall, slipping on cascading water and nearly pitching headfirst down the stairs before righting himself against a railing. One two three huge steps and out into the darkness again, bolting across the field, stupid stupid stupid, of course they were going to react like that, they'd had no idea he was in the barn, plus they'd probably heard more than a few things about big murderous green men on the news—

"Holy fuck we have to go we have to go," he shouted, bursting through the double doors—

—to find the whole crew awake and dressed, cramming supplies into flimsy duffel bags—

—while at the other end of the barn Douglas "Hollywood" Douglas worked on molding wide-eyed surprise into trademark sardonic sneer.

*****

The airship station in Porto resembled a giant Soviet playground, with towering concrete spires and grim dingy chasms between loading plinths that stretched for miles. Tethered to the spires, airships drifted near-imperceptibly in the brisk wind, such that if you stared at them too long you began to feel that the ground was moving beneath you. Everything in sight was gray or black or an extremely jaundiced yellow. Zip, Li, Dr. Alvarez, Vincent, Hollywood, and Tetris, who felt naked beneath his thick impasto of body paint, battled through the teeming crowds to loading dock seventeen, where an airship was scheduled to depart within the hour for New York City.

While the body paint succeeded in de-greening Tetris, it did not render him inconspicuous. It was supposed to be Caucasian skin-colored, but in reality it was closer to orange. Tetris looked either aggressively spray-tanned or afflicted with a horrible skin condition. Based on the berth he was being given, the passersby seemed to have decided on the latter.

"I know you missed me," said Hollywood, throwing an arm around Zip as they walked.

"Sure," said Zip, shrugging out of the arm.

"Partners in crime."

Vincent walked beside them, face hidden behind enormous aviators.

Hollywood popped a bright pink wad of gum. "Li, I don't believe your countryman here has said a word since I arrived."

"I didn't miss you a bit, if you're wondering," said Li.

"You realize I helped save you, right?"

"I would have escaped on my own."

Hollywood snorted, dodging an elderly woman with a pushcart who seemed wholly oblivious to their presence. "Yeah, okay. Buried under forty feet of concrete and bosom-deep in armed guards. Stage a regular old El Chapo kind of deal, I'm sure."

"We had a few ideas," said Dr. Alvarez.

"Science," said Hollywood, seizing on the only fact he knew about Dr. Alvarez, "can only get you so far, gorgeous."

Tetris bristled. "Shut up and keep an eye out."

Hollywood bent back dramatically to stare up at him. "Wow! Here I was thinking you were so deep in the brooding-hero shtick that you wouldn't speak up for at least another couple of days."

Tetris hefted his pack.

Hollywood danced around in front of him. "Look, bud, your twelve-inch green boner for the Doctor is nobody's secret whatsoever."

Tetris stopped walking.

"What?" said Hollywood, hopping from foot to foot with a chimpanzee grin. "Why the smoldering look, hmm? You think you're subtle? I've been here five minutes and I figured it out."

Tetris glimpsed Dr. Alvarez stifling a smile behind her hand.

"You know what," he said, "I did actually miss you, man. I'm thankful you helped me escape, and glad you made it out okay."

Hollywood squinted. The grin vanished. "Umm."

Tetris laid a gentle hand on his shoulder. "I respect and appreciate your friendship. Thank you for everything you've done."

"Think you're clever, huh?"

"Thank you, Hollywood. I am in your debt."

The blond ranger walked the rest of the way in sullen, glowering silence.

24

Tetris was sequestered in narrow quarters usually reserved for the airship's housecleaning staff. Zip and Hollywood had bribed a surly officer for access to the room, which with its bed folded out was barely wide enough for a normal adult male, let alone a hulking green one, to turn 180 degrees. Everyone but Tetris had normal quarters elsewhere on the ship. They came down regularly to visit him, bearing food and stories of adventures on the upper decks, but he couldn't help feeling imprisoned. He folded up the bed to get as much space as possible and paced the room. His shoulders brushed the walls whenever the airship swayed.

Dr. Alvarez kept bringing him books to read (there was a bookstore on deck five), and he kept having to come up with lame excuses for why he hadn't gotten around to opening them. He wasn't in the mood. Instead he spent most of his stationary time gazing out the porthole at the

Atlantic Forest. The canopy was a motionless rug from this height. When clouds obscured his view, he closed his eyes and watched visual feeds from the forest.

The latest vision took him somewhere in the South Pacific, where a ten-story blue heron stalked between the trees with fierce orange eyes beneath black-feathered brows. The creature's beak was a twenty-foot spear. The heron strode crisply to a huge pool of scum-rimmed water.

Lakes were a rarity in the forest, because water tended to drain away through the interlocking debris into the onyx depths. This lake, with the heron stepping carefully along its edge, was actually a rainwater-filled hemisphere of some enormous creature's skull, the jagged bone-edges still protruding through the leaves and dirt in certain spots along the rim.

The heron stopped. For a moment it was still, surveying the water. Then its cocked head began to inch downward, the long neck unfurling, the movement slow and controlled.

When it struck, the heron's head moved so fast that it simply vanished from the sky and reappeared exploding out of the water, reeling back with an alligator speared on the tip of its cruel yellow beak. The reptile's crenellated tail flapped. The heron tilted its head back and tossed the meal down, swallowing in multiple tremoring gulps. It shrugged its wings a little, shifted from foot to foot, and settled itself, long neck reassuming its precise s-curve, ready to strike again.

Sitting on the edge of the folded-out bed, leaning his head on the window, Tetris barely registered the opening of the door.

"Thank God," he said, turning. "I was starv—"

Instead of Li or Dr. Alvarez, a dark-skinned man in a crisp button-up, wide eyes framed by curly hair and a thick beard, stared back at him.

"Pardon me, sir," said the man. He tugged the door closed as fast as he could. Not fast enough, as Tetris lunged across the room to drag him inside.

*****

"Stewart," said Hollywood, "you are not pulling your weight, man."

"Your pal's a real asshole," said Stewart to Zip. They were huddled at one end of the basketball court on the airship's top deck. Their opponents leaned against the far wall, scratching matching chinstraps. One of the opponents had the ball and was spinning it idly on his finger.

"Don't I know it," said Zip.

"Focus!" hissed Hollywood. "Focus! I am not losing to these clowns!"

"Hollywood," said Zip, "we're down fifteen points in a first-to-thirty. I'm pretty sure we lost."

"Quitter."

"Yeah, I quit," said Stewart, who'd introduced himself as an accountant from Maine. Sweat poured down the soft folds of his face.

"No—No. No, you do NOT quit," said Hollywood, grabbing his arm. "And you!" He glowered at Zip. "I thought you'd be good at this."

Zip bristled. "And why's that, huh? Because if you say what I think you're going to say—"

"Never mind."

"Dude. I'm playing with a prosthetic."

"I wish Tetris were here. We need somebody who can dunk."

"I don't understand why you care so much," said Stewart, massaging his wrist where Hollywood had grabbed him. "It's just a game, man."

Hollywood's voice jumped two octaves. "Just a game, he says! Look at them! Look at their cocky faces!"

"Hey idiots," called Li, tossing aside the mesh door, "we've got a situation."

"Not now," said Hollywood. "We're in the middle of a game."

"This is an emergency," said Li. "Involving our friend. The, uh, special one."

Zip dragged Hollywood off the court. They power-walked through the maze of corridors and down the corrugated iron stairs near the back of the ship, Hollywood complaining the whole way.

"I just don't understand what was so important that it couldn't wait ten minutes," he whined.

"If I ever have kids, and they turn out like you, I'm going to smother them," said Li, leaping down the stairs.

They rushed down the hall toward Tetris's room. The door, when it opened, slammed into Tetris's back. He grunted and stepped aside. The dark-skinned man stood, chest puffed out bravely, in the far corner.

"Who's that?" asked Hollywood, up on his tiptoes.

"Move," said Li, shoving Tetris out of the way. When everyone was inside, she crammed the door shut. Dr. Alvarez, sitting on the bed next to the prisoner, brought her legs up to give them room.

"My name is Tejas Ramalingam," said the curly-haired man. "I demand that you release me at once."

"Buddy," said Zip, thinking about the Omphalos Initiative, "why are you here?"

"I'm on my way to a conference in New York," said Mr. Ramalingam.

"No, I mean, why are you in this room?"

"I was looking for a restroom when this gorilla abducted me."

"He opened the door and walked right in," said Tetris. "I figured I couldn't let him go."

"I am an executive and a human being," said Mr. Ramalingam. "I have inalienable rights."

"An executive where?" asked Hollywood, peering around Zip and Li.

"If you must know," said Mr. Ramalingam, "I'm an executive director of sales and marketing for a multinational breakfast foods conglomerate."

"Breakfast foods," said Li.

"Quite. I'm in the toaster pastry division. You'd be surprised all the intricacies that go into—"

"Shut up," said Li.

"What do we do?" asked Tetris.

"You can't just keep him prisoner," said Dr. Alvarez. "Someone will notice that he's gone."

"Someone will most certainly notice that I'm gone," agreed Mr. Ramalingam.

"If we let him go, he'll tell them Tetris is here," said Li.

"I would do no such thing," said Mr. Ramalingam.

"Shut up!"

"I object to your rudeness."

Someone knocked insistently on the door.

"Shit," said Li, turning to Tetris. "Hide."

"Where?"

"Under the bed," said Dr. Alvarez. "We'll stand in front of you."

Tetris wedged himself beneath the fold-out cot.

"Don't say a word," said Li, planting a finger in Mr. Ramalingam's chest. He opened his mouth, saw the look in her eyes, and thought better of whatever he'd intended to say.

Hollywood opened the door. On the other side, a pair of uniformed crewmen stood staring, epaulets shiny and blue.

"What can we do for you gentlemen?" asked Zip.

"What on Earth," said the shorter crewman, whose extremely thick glasses made his eyes look two or three times their actual size.

"We're looking for a Mr. Tejas Rangalingo?" said the taller crewman, hand frozen mid-scratch along his jaw. "His wife sent—we saw on the security cameras that he was—"

"It's Ramalingam," said Mr. Ramalingam over Li's shoulder, prompting her to turn and give him a death glare.

"Who gave you permission to occupy this room?" squeaked the shorter crewman. "These are crew quarters. No passengers—"

Hollywood had his wallet out. "Alright, gentlemen, which currency do we prefer—"

"—my name is Mr. Tejas Ramalingam, I am a citizen of the Republic of India and an executive director of sales and marketing for—"

"—Shut your mouth you little—"

"—is that a bribe? Are you attempting to bribe me?"

"—DON'T HURT ME EEEE THERE IS A GIANT GREEN MAN UNDER THE BED PLEASE HELP ME EEEE—"

"—this is very disorderly, very disorderly conduct indeed, I believe I'll have to call—"

"—no no, I understand, that offer was a bit low, how about let's double it, hmmm? Zip, do you by any chance happen to have your wallet on you? I'm thinking these men are—"

"HELP! I'VE BEEN KIDNAPPED! THEY'RE GOING TO FEED ME TO THE GREEN MAN!"

"—under the bed, is that—is there another person in

257

this room? What's the meaning—"

Soon the two crewmen had joined Mr. Ramalingam beside the window, and things had quieted down substantially.

"Can I come out now?" asked Tetris, his voice muffled. Dr. Alvarez stepped off the bed and flipped it out of the way. Tetris put a hand on his knee and levered himself up.

"The Green Giant," breathed the shorter crewman, eyes filling up his glasses.

"In retrospect, I much preferred 'Green Ranger,'" said Tetris, stretching his cramped neck.

"Who knows you're here?" demanded Li. "How long until they come looking?"

"I'll never tell you anything," said the shorter crewman, raising his chin.

"The captain and the first mate and the quartermaster and the head of security," babbled the tall one, earning ocular daggers from his companion. "Oh God I'm sorry please don't kill me."

"How long do we have?" asked Li.

"Twenty minutes? I don't know! I don't know!"

"Guys," said Dr. Alvarez, "we aren't going to hurt you. We just need to make it to New York without anybody knowing we're on board. Okay? That's all."

"Free us," said Mr. Ramalingam. "We won't breathe a word to anyone."

Hollywood snorted.

"It's not like you have another choice," said Mr. Ramalingam. "You can only fit so many kidnapees in this room."

The room was indeed growing extremely crowded. Tetris yearned for fresh air.

"Here's the plan," said Li. "Tetris, stay here. Doc, retrieve the body paint and get Tetris suited up, just in case. Everybody else: we're going to the bridge."

Just like that, the room emptied out. Tetris, alone again, pushed a hand through his hair and exhaled heavily. Then he popped the bed, sat down, and cracked open one of the books from Dr. Alvarez.

25

"I've been thinking about the plane crash," said Dr. Alvarez as she rubbed body paint on the back of Tetris's neck.

"What about it?"

"'Airplane engines don't just explode' is common knowledge, I feel. Especially on carefully maintained government aircraft."

"That feels," he rumbled, "super good, by the way."

"So obviously the plane was sabotaged."

"Oh, obviously, yeah. Uh huh."

"The question is who sabotaged it."

"Hmm."

Her hands retreated. Tetris sighed.

"Whoever it was," she said, "they had access to the

runway, right? The plane landed, picked us up, soared away. Blew up in midair."

"China," he said. "Russia?"

"That was my first thought. But if news got out—that they tried to kill the Secretary of State—think about the disaster that would be. Why take the risk? If they wanted you dead, why not murder you in your sleep?"

"Me?"

"So I assumed terrorism. But I've been doing some research, and it seems like nobody took credit. Everyone seems to think it was a malfunction. It was made to look like a malfunction. Which only leaves one possibility."

Vincent Chen bulldozed into the room. "What the fuck is going on?"

Tetris rose. "You ever heard of knocking?"

"Everyone is missing," said Vincent. "People are saying the ship's been hijacked. The captain came over the intercom and told us to stay in our rooms." He turned and spat quickly into the hall. "And you're back in body paint."

"Vince," said Dr. Alvarez, "take it easy."

In the expression Vincent directed at Dr. Alvarez, a familiar internal battle unfolded. His lip curled and uncurled like a worm trapped on the sidewalk.

"Walk with us," she said.

They made their way to the bridge, Vincent prowling, Tetris's long arms swinging at his side. When they knocked, the heavy door swung open, and Zip ushered them through.

"Word is out," said Dr. Alvarez. "What happened?"

"Housecleaning caught me unpacking my gun," said Hollywood, leaning on the console beside the captain, whose trim blue-lined hat was sorely askew. "The lady ran before I could add her to our collection."

He gestured toward the corner where six crew members and one Indian breakfast pastry executive sported matching scowls. Under Li's raptor gaze, none of them seemed inclined to budge.

"What's to stop the passengers from notifying the authorities?" asked Dr. Alvarez.

"We disabled the satellite internet," said Li, nodding at a panel that showed signs of repeated bludgeoning. A battle-scarred fire extinguisher lay nearby. "And until we're closer to shore, they can't get signal to use cell phones."

The captain swallowed hard. His Adam's apple jumped up and down.

Hollywood scratched himself under the chin with the barrel of his gun. "We've got our buddy here making regular announcements. 'Apologies for the broken internet,' 'Remain in your rooms until the turbulence subsides,' 'Dinner canceled but we'll send housekeeping around with some extra mints,' et cetera. He's got a great voice. Dude should be calling ball games."

"Please," said the captain, "put the gun away. We're cooperating."

He really did have a deep and sonorous voice. Hollywood shrugged and stuck the pistol in his waistband.

"We would like to avoid hurting anyone," said Li.

One of the prisoners, whose face was sprouting purple lumps in several places, snorted.

Li shrugged. "Anyone else, I mean."

"What happened to him?" asked Tetris.

"Our friend here fancied himself a kickboxer," said Li primly. She examined her knuckles.

"I'm a black belt," said the bruised prisoner defensively.

Li faked toward him, shoulder jutting, and the prisoner flung himself into the arms of his comrades.

Vincent blew air through pursed lips. "Hijacking. I believe I draw the line at hijacking."

"Nobody asked your opinion," said Hollywood.

"You're committing a federal crime," said Vincent. "This is terrorism. There's no going back from here."

"Oh, come on," said Li. "We'll let them go when we arrive."

"Doctor," said Vincent, "you don't have to be a part of this."

Dr. Alvarez gave him a crooked smile. "It's way too late for that, Vince."

"This is wrong," he said.

"If we stop now, we'll fall right into the FBI's arms," said Zip.

"If you're innocent, you have nothing to fear."

"We're not innocent," said Tetris. "But neither are they."

Vincent didn't look at him, just pounded a fist into an open palm, turned, and thrust the heavy steel door out of his way. It slammed shut behind him.

"I am wondering," said Tetris when the silence had curdled, "how we intend to keep this a secret when we get within cell range."

"We'll be long gone by then," said Li.

*****

That night, Tetris and Zip had first shift watching the prisoners.

"There's something I've been meaning to tell you," said Zip.

"Whatever it is, don't worry about it."

"We met your dad, man. Back when everybody thought you were dead."

Tetris didn't know how to respond, so he didn't say anything at all.

After a while Zip shifted, crossing his prosthetic leg beneath the other. "I liked him, actually."

"Hmm."

"Hollywood didn't want to take him. Your dad couldn't pay, obviously. But I paid for him. I don't know if I'm afraid of you being mad about that, or what."

"I'm not mad."

Zip wiped his mouth on the back of his hand. "He cares about you, I think."

"That's what you think?"

"It's none of my business."

One of the prisoners snored like a row of laundromat

dryers. Tetris battled an urge to kick him.

"So are you telling me this," said Tetris, "because you know where he is, and you want me to visit him? Something like that?"

"I just felt like it was a weird thing to keep from you. Like, hey, I met your dad and almost got him killed, and never told you about it."

Tetris cracked his neck once in each direction.

"Everybody on that trip died except him and Hollywood," said Zip.

"Tougher than he looks."

"Runs in the family, huh?"

"Some of us, anyway."

*****

The New York City skyline was a blip on the horizon when Tetris and the others stepped off the airship's emergency exit deck and into empty air. Tumbling, Tetris extended his arms and legs and thrust his face into the wind. The parachute and gear were a reassuring weight on his back. Finally some action!

He rolled to look up at the others as they plummeted after him. Beating his chest, he unleashed a joyous animal roar, but the wind carried it away. He turned his attention back to the fast-approaching canopy.

Welcome home, said the forest.

Tetris grinned so hard that the edges of his wind-seared face began to hurt.

They floated down like dandelion seeds on plump white parachutes. The treetops, which looked so soft from above, proved to be full of grasping branches and whisking leaf edges. Dragons and spiders scampered through the canopy, rooting out any wildlife likely to prove dangerous to the forest's guests. As Tetris unhitched from his parachute and fell sure-footed to a branch immediately below, he closed his eyes and breathed deep. The fecund oxygen-rich air that filled his lungs was nothing like the harsh cigarette smoke of the airship port or the crisp but flavorless air of the Portuguese countryside. This air was alive.

Why the airship had carried an arsenal of ranger gear in a fusty cargo hold was anybody's guess, but Tetris and the others were certainly grateful for the oversight. Once everyone had landed, they rappelled smartly to the forest floor.

"I didn't realize how much I missed this," said Zip, testing his prosthetic against a fallen branch.

Everyone seemed to share the sentiment. They stood for a while and listened. The air swam with pollen and golden motes. A pillbug poked its head out and wiggled antennae at them. Tetris pressed a palm against a mossy trunk, reveling in the tree's smoky aroma and implacable firmness. The buzz of tiny insects came in waves, an ambient lullaby. Somewhere just out of sight, dragons crashed and caroused, occasionally issuing half-hearted shrieks. The spiders had retreated.

Hurry, said the forest.

"Let's go," said Tetris. They were still fugitives. China and Brazil were still dumping defoliants on the canopy. And the invisible cosmic cataclysm was still grinding toward them, inevitable as the sun's eventual implosion. Back in Seattle, his old answering machine was probably still blinking, crammed full of unanswered messages from his father.

"Hey," said Li a few minutes later, jogging up beside him. Her tight-strapped pack bounced on her shoulders. "Slow down. We can't keep up."

Tetris turned and saw them straggling along, Zip limping in the rear.

"Sorry," he said. "I got distracted."

"Let me lead for a while," she said, and reached up to pat him on the shoulder. "Keep Zip company."

Tetris stood aside and let Hollywood and Dr. Alvarez pass.

"You fuckers better not slow down for me," growled Zip.

"No matter what," said Tetris, "this can't be slower than last time."

Zip stuck his arms out to balance as his prosthetic foot twisted on a loose stone. Tetris caught his elbow.

"Don't touch me," said Zip, tugging his arm free.

"Let me know if you want a piggy-back ride," said Tetris brightly.

The reply, a list of unsanitary objects and corresponding orifices Tetris was invited to insert them into, brought a smile to his worn green face.

26

It was four-thirty a.m. and the sun had just begun to suggest a rise out of the green expanse behind them. Several miles north, a flock of dragons distracted the Coast Guard. Tetris, coat of paint flecking, led the way between spotlights and up the sandy slope. They hurried across the no-man's-land and ducked under the black and yellow bar of a Coast Guard checkpoint. The checkpoint's sole occupant snored in a teetering chair.

Atlantic City. Tetris crossed a deserted boardwalk under three-story crimson letters. The streets beyond were empty. The air was cold and still except for occasional gusts with fluoride edges. A truck rumbled by, trailing cartoonish curls of exhaust.

The few pedestrians in view wrote them off in a single sliding glance. A raccoon rustling in a dumpster poked its head out, deemed them no threat, and returned to scavenging. Even the clouds seemed shriveled from the cold. They were looking for a motel when Zip spotted a familiar figure on the far side of the street.

"George!"

Tetris snapped around. Skyscrapers and parking decks folded down like scenery in a pop-up book. His father looked both ways and crossed the street.

"Thomas," said George Aphelion, "you have to leave. They're coming."

Oh yeah, said the forest, *I forgot to tell you about him.*

Tetris, stepping backward, slipped on the curb and stumbled into the street. Something hummed past his ear. The flat crack of the gunshot arrived afterward, and as Tetris regained his footing he saw his father collapsing, spinning to the pavement and clawing at unconcerned air—

Tetris scooped him up and hurtled behind a parked car. The sidewalk kicked up splinters as a second shot missed. Although he felt no pain, Tetris knew he'd bit hard into his tongue.

George was whiter than bone. A darkening blotch

stained his side.

Li skidded around the corner.

"Stay with him," said Tetris.

Li ripped her pack open. Glass sprayed overhead from a third shot. George, eyes closed, remained still. Tetris rooted in his pack.

"The rooftop," said Li as her hands whisked across George, tearing his shirt open, bandages flying off their rolls. She bit off a length of tape.

"That's my dad," said Tetris.

George mouthed something.

"Fuck," said Tetris, trying to convert the tears to something more useful. His muscles hummed. "Fuck. Fuck."

"It's a scratch," said Li, bandaging the gash. "Tetris. He's fine. It only nicked him."

Tetris wrenched the grapple gun out of his pack and lunged around the corner. There—a flash of sun on scope. Gargoyles leered from the edge of the roof. Tetris raised the grapple gun and fired.

He crossed the void to the rooftop in a single breath. The wind tore tears from his eyes. He reached the gargoyle and grasped its curled stone tail. Fingers raw on time-scarred stone, he went over the lip like a spider. The sniper turned, hefting his awkward rifle, the bipod swinging slack beneath the barrel.

Tetris dove. He caught the man's leg and shoved him back as the rifle discharged overhead. The man released his gun, which toppled over the edge, and struck Tetris on the back of the head. Falling hard on one hand, Tetris righted himself, but the man was already circling, knife flitting out of its sheath.

The man dodged Tetris's reaching hand and opened a gash along his arm. Tetris landed a shoulder to the exposed chest, but his assailant only danced back. The knife came flying in again, ready to bury itself in green abdominal flesh. Tetris caught the hand.

He tried to snap the wrist, but the man rolled with the motion somehow and fired off a kick as he went, foot landing hard against Tetris's temple. As blood pumped from the gash on his inner arm, Tetris grabbed for the man's neck. Again he dodged.

The roof was empty except for a concrete structure behind the assassin, its entryway doorstopped by a folded newspaper.

The assassin shoulder-faked and smiled when Tetris flinched. Above the black turtleneck, his skin was pink. His breath hung crystalline in the air.

Tetris snorted a thundercloud and charged.

He swung and swung, the blows firing off fast and unrestrained, but the man refused to be touched, sneaking in a slash here and there as he ducked and slid. Tetris pulled away, panting. Blood flowed from several cuts, stinging in the grime and body paint. One was just above his eye. He wiped the blood away.

Still the man jeered, silent.

He's playing with you, said the forest.

"Real fucking helpful," said Tetris, spitting blood.

Then he thought about it for a second.

Again he closed the gap, winding up for a haymaker. As the assassin shifted, Tetris abandoned the punch and snapped his torso around. His left fist zipped electric-fast to fill the corridor of space the assassin's dodge had taken him to—

Ribs buckled. The assassin bent almost in half and began at once to recover, the knife slashing around, no kidding this time, aimed at the jugular—and Tetris stepped out of the deadly steel arc. Struck a hard flat blow that snapped the assassin's head back.

That was the opening. Tetris grabbed the wrist and broke it for real this time. His knee met the man's hard midriff as the knife skittered away. Blood spattered from Tetris's wounds as he flung the man against the narrow edge of the door. The impact was so great that Tetris momentarily lost his hold. He drove a knee into the man's stomach as he fell, feeling soft innards give way. Rage screamed in his thunking skull.

The man struggled to his knees. Blood poured from his mouth. Tetris reared back and...

The assassin blinked, waiting.

Tetris dropped his fist. "Who are you?"

The assassin didn't respond. Sirens shrieked. Tetris peered over the edge as cop cars raced around the corner. Li and the others were nowhere to be seen.

Down the stairs, urged the forest. *They may not know you're up here yet.*

A flash of movement and Tetris whirled, but the

assassin wasn't headed for him. Like a demented stork, he staggered to the railing and flung himself off. A thin ribbon of blood trailed after him. Tetris watched him hit the pavement.

"Holy shit."

There's no time.

"You brought my dad," said Tetris as he rushed down the stairs. He wiped his hands on his shirt. Body paint came away with the blood, revealing splotches of green skin.

He wanted to help. I linked to him in the Pacific.

"Is he going to die?"

Silence.

Tetris covered flight after flight. On the bottom floor he paused, unsure which route to take. A pair of hands reached out and grabbed his arm.

"This way," hissed Hollywood, and ran.

They weaved down a hallway and blasted through a swinging door. Beyond was a kitchen, all brushed steel and dangling knives, the narrow aisles bustling with workers. Tetris accidentally knocked a pot out of someone's hands. Noodles smashed in steaming heaps on the blue and white tile.

Then they were outside. Hollywood was fast, had always been fast, and Tetris found that he could really unleash, stretch his legs and not worry about leaving the blond ranger behind. They flew down an alley as police sirens careened off the walls.

"Who was that?" asked Hollywood.

"No idea," said Tetris, "but he's dead."

He felt the words leave his mouth, but somehow they still sounded like they originated from some point outside his body. They paused behind a dumpster as a taxi rolled quietly past.

"Hey," shouted Hollywood, running into the street with his arms waving.

"What about the others?" asked Tetris as the cab slowed.

"What about them?"

"We can't just leave them."

"Can, will, and are about to," said Hollywood, ducking into the cab.

A cop car screamed across a distant intersection, lights flashing, heading back the way they'd come.

"Last chance," said Hollywood, reaching for the door. Tetris caught it and tossed his gear inside.

The turbaned cabby proffered a tall-toothed smile. "Where to, sirs?"

"Pottsville, Pennsylvania," said Hollywood.

The driver blinked. His bushy mustache wriggled. "Too far."

"How's two thousand bucks sound?"

Soon they were on the expressway, roaring northwest.

"Where are we going?" asked Tetris.

"I know a guy," said Hollywood. "We can lay low at his place for a while."

Tetris shifted, trying to position his legs so blood could reach his tingling feet. "How long's the drive?"

"Three hours, sirs," said the cab driver. "Music?"

"No," said Tetris.

"Yes, please," said Hollywood.

The driver reached for the knob, paused, looked at Tetris in the rear view, and retracted his hand. Tetris showed his canines.

"Hey," said Hollywood. "I'm the one paying the bill."

So they listened to the radio. Pop music. The driver hummed along. Tetris leaned against the window and watched the highway unfurl.

"Look, shithead, your dad's going to be fine," said Hollywood.

The trees that weren't already bare were changing, an intermittent frenzy of orange and red. It seemed like half the trucks they passed were hauling lumber. Tetris pinched his arm, twisting the green skin until it turned blue-black.

Every hour or so, they faded out of radio range, and the driver had to fiddle with the dial to find something new. They listened to country, R&B, and another pop station before finally the sign for Pottsville appeared overhead.

"Where do I drop you off?" asked the driver as they cruised down Pottsville's narrow streets. It was 9 a.m. and the residents of the town were walking their dogs down rows of identical red-roofed houses.

"I'm starving," said Hollywood. "What's that say? Right there's fine."

The diner was packed with white-haired, suspendered working men. Waitresses sailed through the aisles with sloshing pots of coffee. Tetris and Hollywood tossed their gear into a booth and slid in after it. Everything was bathed in the saturated yellow light of a courthouse snack shop.

"What'll you have, honey?" asked the gum-munching waitress, plucking a pen from behind her ear.

"Coffee, please," said Hollywood. "Four eggs. Bacon. And sausage. Do you guys have blueberry pancakes? I'll have those too, thanks. Extra butter."

The waitress scrawled three quick hieroglyphs and turned to Tetris. "What about you, hon?"

"Bacon and eggs, please," said Tetris. "And a large Coke."

The best that could be said about the food was that it was warm. Still, it beat the forest tubers they'd been eating for the past week, so their plates were cleaned in minutes. Tetris emptied his soda in two gulps and asked for a refill. Stole one of Hollywood's pancakes when he was in the bathroom, then ordered a stack for himself.

"Y'all have a pay phone?" asked Hollywood when the waitress came to collect their dishes.

"Round the corner at the dollar store," said the waitress. Hollywood tipped her a fifty.

It had begun to warm up a bit. The sun shone out of a pallid blue void. Hollywood watched a young mother push a stroller down the opposite sidewalk.

"Oo-wee," he said, blowing into his hands and rubbing them. His nose was pink.

More than anything else, Tetris wanted a shower. He

searched the windows of every house they passed. Even walking through a real-life Norman Rockwell painting, he couldn't shake the feeling that someone was waiting to leap out of the bushes with an Uzi.

"Hey Dicer," said Hollywood after he'd dialed. "Need a favor."

The voice that came crackling through the receiver was rich and expressive, but Tetris couldn't make out a word it said.

"Pottsville," said Hollywood. "Down the street from, uh, Gramma's Family Diner." He paused, listening. "Yeah, no, I didn't try the roast beef, but I saw some other folks— yeah, no, I hear you. Looked like a winner."

"Who is this guy?" asked Tetris when Hollywood hung up.

"You'll like him," said Hollywood.

Thirty minutes later, Dicer roared up in a pickup truck the size of a bulldozer. He leapt down to greet Hollywood with a handshake that promptly turned into a hug.

"Douglas Squared," said Dicer. "Way too long, comrade."

As quick as he'd wrapped Hollywood in a hug, Dicer sprang back, hopping lightly from toe to toe. He was six and a half feet of dark rolling muscle, bald, with a wreath of curly hair along his cheeks and beneath his chin. His eyes were big and jolly, and his nose looked to have been broken at least four or five times. He wore a tired gray muscle shirt with "MILF Hunter" in faded red letters.

"Jim," said Hollywood, "this is my buddy, Tetris."

"You're a big one," said Dicer. "Ever think about MMA?"

"I don't know if they have a weight class for him," said Hollywood. "Let's split."

They bombed along Pottsville's roads, Tetris in the back seat grabbing the handle over the door every time they hit a curve. Something that sounded like a bunch of steel chains clattered in the truck bed.

"What have you got back there?" asked Tetris.

"Bunch of steel chains," said Dicer. "So what is it this time, Douglas? Y'all rob a nursing home?"

"Yeah," said Hollywood, "we're on a string of nursing home robberies. They call us the Denture Desperados. Got a sack full of fake teeth right here. Just waiting for things to cool down before I flip 'em on the prosthodontic black market."

Douglas looked at him gravely.

"Yeah," he said, "I've been there." He brightened, slaloming into the oncoming lane to zoom past a school bus. "Well, no fear. It's a great time to hole up in the country. Hunting's great! Fishing's great! Yesterday I caught a snapper turtle!"

Hollywood unwrapped a cube of pink bubble gum. "They have those up here?"

"Evidently."

They were out of the city now, bumping along a rugged road.

"Where are you from, big guy?"

It took Tetris a minute to realize the question was

directed at him. "Indianapolis."

"No shit. I love Indy."

Tetris curled and uncurled a hand. "Why's that?"

"Cheese steak. Best cheese steaks in the Midwest."

"Cheese steak?"

"That's correct."

"I wasn't aware—"

"No, they have them, you just have to know where to look."

Eventually they took an exit and drove half an hour down a narrow highway lined closely with trees that had discarded most of their leaves. Then they came to an even smaller road, unmarked, that led into the forest. The road wound back and forth, passing isolated residences, narrowing all the time, until finally it turned to gravel. Onward the great truck roared, its mighty tires kicking up stones.

Dicer's house, on the edge of a kidney-shaped lake, had big glass windows and a truly gigantic satellite dish mounted on the roof.

"You have a dog, Dice?" asked Hollywood. "This looks like the kind of property that has three, four dogs, minimum."

"Nope," said Dicer. "I used to have a cat. Woke up one night and he was on my chest, staring into my eyes, three inches from my face. Freaked me out, man. Never had a pet since."

Inside, Dicer beelined for the fridge and pulled out a carton of orange juice, unscrewed the cap, and glugged.

Tetris and Hollywood stood and watched. When he was finished, Dicer crushed the carton and belched.

"Man," he shouted. "That is fresh SQUEEZED!"

"Can I get some of that?" asked Hollywood.

"Sure," said Dicer, tossing him an unopened carton. Hollywood nearly dropped it. Carton number two sailed Tetris's way, and he snagged it out of the air with one huge hand.

"What happened to that finger?" asked Dicer, pointing.

"I lost it," said Tetris.

Dicer squinted at him for a second. Then he laughed and slapped his belly, producing a sound like a trout smacking against a concrete wall.

"You," he whooped. "You crack me up!"

*****

That night, Dicer and Hollywood watched an entire trilogy of sword-and-sorcery movies. Technically, Tetris was there too, although he kept tuning out, and didn't really follow the action. Something about an old guy in a white bathrobe, with a stick that made light, was what he remembered afterward. Dicer had most of the lines memorized, and liked to shout them, especially the grumpy dwarf's. Hollywood was the kind of incessant movie talker Tetris despised, but Dicer seemed to love the snarky commentary. The two friends finished by 2 a.m. and went straight to bed. Tetris slipped out the back door and walked around the lake.

The night was cold. Tetris walked briskly, and when that wasn't enough to keep his body temperature up, broke into a run. He whipped through the trees, reveling in the snapping chill. A deer crossed his path, eyes glowing under the moon. Tetris thought about chasing it, but straying from the lake was likely to get him lost, so he left it alone and continued his run.

When he made it back to the house, he was huffing and gasping, sweat flying off his body. He went inside and took a long shower. Dirt, dried blood, and body paint washed away, swirling around the drain. Long after Tetris was clean, the debris that had crusted his body kept circling. He stayed in the shower, sucking deep breaths of steam with his eyes closed, until the debris was all gone.

Out of the shower, Tetris saw his clean green body in the mirror and cursed. They hadn't told Dicer. But the body paint was in Dr. Alvarez's pack. He'd just have to do his best to explain the verdant complexion when their host awoke.

In the morning Dicer padded out of his bedroom and nodded at Tetris. He pulled out another carton of orange juice—the fridge was packed with them—and chugged half of it.

"Fresh squeezed," he said, gently twisting the cap back onto the carton.

"Good morning," said Tetris.

"You are green," said Dicer. His bulging pecs were barely restrained by a yellow muscle shirt with the silhouette of a rubber duck on the front.

"Yes I am."

Dicer shrugged, belched, and traded the orange juice for an extra-large carton of eggs, which he set on the counter. He retrieved a block of cheese and a sheaf of bacon as well, placing them next to the eggs, and grabbed a gigantic skillet that hung beside a framed image of a four-armed cartoon pocket monster.

"I do not understand even a single thing about you," said Tetris.

"What was that?" asked Dicer in a deep and pleasant voice. He cracked eggs into the skillet one after the other, tossing the shells in the trash, *bam* toss *bam* toss *bam*. "We start training today, or what?"

"Training?"

"Comrade," said Dicer, gaze fierce beneath thick eyebrows, "I can spot a fighter a mile away."

Tetris looked out the floor-to-ceiling windows at the grasping, leafless trees, the birds flitting in the upper branches, and the lake, a still sheet of glass.

Could hardly hurt, said the forest, before fading away again.

Tetris ran a finger along the ridge of scar tissue above his eye. Eggs and bacon popped and sizzled in the pan. The air was full of greasy breakfast smells. He allowed himself a long, deep sigh.

"Okay," he said, "I'm in."

27

The basement was luminous and carpeted with thick blue mats. Tetris thought they were going to start by going over moves, or at least discussing what MMA was, but instead Dicer went straight to beating the everliving shit out of him. The blows were designed to show that Dicer could have hurt him, rather than to cause actual injury, but there were a lot of them. Tetris, for all his lunges and swings, never landed a solid strike.

Dicer downstairs was completely different from Dicer upstairs. In the basement, he never spoke. He was expressionless, his eyes half-lidded and saurian, his legs in constant liquid motion. Sometimes he dodged a blow, caught Tetris's arm, and flung him to the mat. It was like fighting a cyclone of smoke. Hollywood watched from the corner, leaning on a pendulous punching bag, and occasionally laughed or let loose a hearty "Hoo-wee!"

They kept going after lunch. The mats were cool and crisp beneath Tetris's bare feet, but they soon grew slippery with sweat. The basement filled with the hiss-slide of feet on vinyl and the wet thwacking of fists against green flesh.

The morning had been a maelstrom, Tetris throwing out swing after swing and getting punished for every one. By three o'clock, the pace had slowed considerably. Tetris, clothed in bruises, his mouth coated with sweat-salt, felt like curling up at the bottom of a well. He hung back and considered each move. Dicer paced happily. He didn't seem to mind the slower tempo. It certainly didn't prevent him from landing hits.

Hollywood propped his chair back and slept. A wad of gum was wedged in the side of his open mouth. Tetris, jumbled up, rolled his shoulders and raised his fists. He fired off a careful tap, watching Dicer's hands. Dicer took the weak hit and feinted a reprisal, but didn't follow through. Tetris caught sinewy motion in his peripheral vision, weight transferring subtly to the balls of Dicer's feet. He stepped back, raising his hands in front of his face, as Dicer knifed left and rebounded, striking briskly with one fist and then the other. Tetris's arms cushioned the blows. He pressed forward. The swift response took Dicer by surprise, creating an ephemeral opening. Green hands lashed out. One of them caught Dicer's midriff, eliciting a grunt, but by the time the second hand arrived, Dicer was already compensating, swiveling away, and Tetris's knuckles slid harmlessly off knobby muscle.

"Good," said Dicer, voice as orotund as ever despite hours of disuse. His fearsome fists came down. Two loping steps took him to the towel rack. "Good!"

After a moment, Tetris relaxed. His shoulder blades had been clenched so tightly that they screamed white-hot when he released them. He moved unsteadily to the rack and procured a towel. In the most inaccessible crevices of his body, muscles hissed and twinged and sang. Dicer skipped across the room and snapped Hollywood with the tip of his sweat-drenched towel. The blond ranger flailed awake, lost his balance, and toppled out of the teetering chair. Dicer laughed from the belly and spun the damp fabric like a propeller.

"Motherfuc--" choked Hollywood, "I swallowed my gum--"

Dicer chased him, towel snip-snapping, to the stairs. Hollywood yelped and whooped and booked it out of the basement.

"Is that it?" asked Tetris. "Is that supposed to be a lesson?"

Dicer turned around and stuck a contemplative finger in the sodden curls of his beard. "Pardon me?"

Tetris threw his drenched towel in the hamper and tugged a replacement off the rack. "You didn't teach me anything."

Dicer's shrug was an avalanche. "If that's what you think," he said.

That night Tetris took a kayak out to the middle of the lake and sat bobbing in the dendriform wind. The moon overhead was near-full, a pale orb with a neat bite out of it. As his muscle fibers knit back together, he leaned over the edge and stared into the depths. Submerged a hand. It was liquid nitrogen cold, but he held his hand under the surface until the fingers grew brittle and pinpricked with minuscule needles. The water was pure impenetrable black. It was the kind of water that suggested something huge and menacing lurking just beneath the surface.

He spent a while thinking about what that huge thing might be. A creature with slits for eyes and a mouth big enough to swallow the kayak. Behind the teeth like mountain spires, a gullet of bone-white rings. Smooth black skin, firm but pliable, cartilage, fins protruding at extreme angles, and a mighty broad blade of a tail.

He closed his eyes and stowed his hands in his armpits.

Guilt and fear roiled like water snakes in his gut. Thinking about certain things made the sensation worse. So he tried not to think about those things. But there were so many of them, now. The impending invasion. The Omphalos Initiative. The carnage in Portugal. His father. The misplaced terror on the face of the Spanish farmer. The knowledge that most of the world thought he, Tetris Aphelion, was a murderer. The fact that, in a way, he kind of was.

After a while he turned and paddled back to the house. Meanwhile the spilled liquids that made up his bruises, red and black and yellow, sucked back into the network of veins and slimy sacs from which they'd burst, like the water sucking through the teeming pebbles along the shore.

If Dicer had been unfazed by Tetris's verdant skin, he was at least impressed by the speed at which it shed the previous day's beating.

"Your bruises," he said, bustling over to lift Tetris's arm and examine it from all angles. He pulled up Tetris's shirt, too, head darting down to flit eyes across every inch of unblemished torso. "Wow. Wow! *Wow!*"

"Get off," said Tetris, and pulled away.

"Guess I don't have to go easy on you, then," said Dicer, retreating to take an enormous bite out of a bright green apple.

Things went on like that for a week, Dicer wordlessly pummeling Tetris during the day, the forest doing its best to repair the damage overnight. An elbow-jointed pipe in the corner of the basement's ceiling dripped condensation with metronomic regularity. Eventually Dicer decided that the silent thwacking had served its purpose, and began to teach directly, sparse instructions delivered in a hushed, gravelly tone. They began to incorporate grappling: clinching and takedowns, escapes and submissions. Every time Tetris thought he had a handle on the basics, Dicer introduced something new.

As the days went by, the words they spoke grew fewer and farther between. Tetris thought less and less about the world and his mission to save it. There were still six years to go. He wondered where Li and the others had gone. A strange lethargy quelled any desire to seek them out. Where would he even begin to look?

One day, Tetris and Dicer emerged from the basement to find the lakefront vanishing beneath a fluffy blanket of snow.

When the novelty of watching Tetris get bludgeoned wore off, all Hollywood did was sleep. He slept out on the porch in thick winter clothes borrowed from Dicer, obscured except for the puff of his breath. He slept on the couch in front of the grumbling television. He slept wherever a sunbeam came falling through the tall windows when the gray clouds parted. Some days he woke only for meals, or, when the food ran out, to make a run to the grocery store in Dicer's truck.

"You ever hear the parable of the Houston man and the alligator?" asked Dicer as they toweled off one afternoon. He had a fat purple crescent under his eye where an errant strike had caught him.

"No."

"There's an eighteen-foot alligator living under a bridge."

Tetris pressed his toes against the wall and leaned, stretching his calf.

"A Houston man comes up to the bridge with his girlfriend and takes off his shirt. He wants to go for a swim. And an older man walks by at that exact moment, right? And the older man says--"

"Don't jump in there, mayne," interjected Tetris in a laughable approximation of a Southern accent. "There's a big ol' gater under that there bridge."

"But he doesn't listen," said Dicer.

"He most certainly does not."

"'Fuck that alligator,' he says, and jumps in."

Drip, went the pipe in the corner. Drip. Drip.

"I'm guessing it eats him."

"First Texas alligator fatality in two hundred years."

Tetris touched an earlobe gingerly, trying to discern if a blow from Dicer had knocked it loose. "Moral: obey your elders?"

Dicer shrugged and headed up the stairs. "'Don't fuck with alligators,' is what I figured."

That night, around two o'clock a.m., someone knocked on the door.

Tetris went over. His legs were stiff and sore. After a few moments, he twisted the handle and pulled it open.

On the porch stood Vincent Chen, his cold-reddened face wreathed with scraggly hair. A pistol in his right hand dangled toward the earth.

"Hello," said Vincent.

"Hi," said Tetris.

"I found your cab driver," said Vincent.

Snowflakes drifted across the headlights of his parked sedan.

"Then the pay phone you used in Pottsville."

Tetris leaned against the doorframe. He felt like he was ten feet outside his body, viewing the scene through a foggy window.

"Turn yourself in," said Vincent. "No handcuffs necessary. Just come with me."

Tetris shook his shaggy head. The car's headlights

turned themselves off, shrouding Vincent in shadow.

"I called the feds," said Vincent in a hoarse voice. "They'll be here soon."

Tetris thought about closing the door and running out the back, then fleeing into the forest. Just the thought made him tired. He closed his eyes and saw for a moment the dead-eyed face of the assassin on the rooftop.

"Vince," he said.

When he opened his eyes the pistol was pointed at him.

"I'm sorry," said Vincent, sounding like he really meant it, "but I have to do the right thing."

Break his arm, said the forest.

Tetris thought of the soldiers on the Portuguese coast and in the Omphalos base. Blood seeping into cracks and crevices out of which it could never be scrubbed. He left the door open and walked back inside.

"I'm not kidding," said Vincent, and followed.

Dicer stepped out of the bedroom with a shotgun braced against his shoulder. There was a horrific crash. Vincent bounced hard off the edge of the door, pistol flying from his grasp. Tetris crossed the room before it landed.

"Hold your fire!"

Vincent's abdomen was a ragged mess. Feathers from his ruptured jacket fluttered in the air.

"No can do," said Dicer, although he lowered the shotgun.

Vincent's lips pulled back from his teeth. He rolled away, or tried to, when Tetris touched him.

"They're coming," Vincent choked.

"We have to get him to the hospital," said Tetris, struggling out of his shirt. He wadded it up and pressed it to the wound. Wind ripped through the doorway, a fusillade of frozen daggers.

"*Who's* coming?" demanded Dicer.

Hollywood emerged from his own bedroom. He stood, blinking, and threaded his arms into a heavy sweatshirt. "This fucker again?"

Tetris found Vincent's keys. "I'm taking him to the hospital."

Dicer paced, running a hand over his bald dome. "He talking about who I think he's talking about?"

"Dicer, you have to come along. You have to show me where the hospital is."

"Nope," said Dicer. "They shoot guys like me on sight."

Tetris flew to his bag, teeth jumping from the cold, and pulled on layers as fast as he could. "Hollywood?"

The blond ranger sucked his teeth. "We oughta be headed in the opposite direction."

"He's going to die."

Hollywood blinked. "I thought you hated this guy."

"He's going to die, Hollywood."

"He pulled a gun on you."

"He needs our help."

"Route 66," said Dicer from the bedroom, over the sound of drawers being ransacked, "take exit 85, and follow the signs."

He emerged in a pink tank top and shrugged into a

coat, then slung a duffel bag over his shoulder.

"Good luck," he said.

Tetris picked Vincent up and waded into the swirling snow.

The agent's sleek black sedan was parked beside the mailbox. Tetris lowered him into the passenger seat, fastened the belt, and sprinted around, keys jangling.

"C'mon c'mon c'mon," he said, gunning the engine and spinning the wheel hand over hand. They fishtailed out of the driveway, nearly slamming into the trees on the far side. Vincent groaned.

"Oh, God," he said.

"Stay with me, buddy," said Tetris. "Which direction are the FBI guys coming from? Can we meet them halfway?"

The seatbelt kept Vincent from folding over completely, but his arms were wrapped tight around his darkening midsection.

"Okay, that's okay, no big deal," said Tetris, peering at a sign as they whipped by. The tree trunks were red under the headlights. Vincent slumped against his belt.

"Hey," said Tetris, prodding his shoulder. "Hey. Talk to me."

Vincent shuddered and pulled away. "What?"

"Tell me something. Tell me a story."

Vincent pressed his skull against the headrest.

"My brother," he said. "Oh God. My brother."

"What about him?"

Vincent coughed. "I was a cop."

"You mentioned that."

Yellow dashes snapped past beneath a thin veneer of snow.

"I miss him," said Vincent quietly.

Tetris glanced over. "I miss my brother too," he said.

Vincent didn't respond. His eyes were closed.

Suddenly the road was alive with blistering white-yellow lights. Muscular black vans swarmed everywhere. Snowflakes sprang in the high beams as Tetris jammed the brakes. As they shuddered to a halt, he shifted into park. Vans swerved into place behind and in front. Their exhaust pipes belched black smoke.

Tetris lowered his window.

"All right," he shouted. "You got me. I'm coming quietly."

In the driver-side window appeared the sneering face of the scarred torturer from Portugal.

Tetris began a lunge but was stopped by the cold barrel of an enormous revolver against his forehead. Omphalos soldiers in heavy gear dispersed into the trees. Their boots left harsh marks in the snow.

"I don't believe we were ever properly introduced," said a silky voice behind him.

Tetris removed his forehead carefully from the pistol. He knew the voice. It was the voice that had come over the intercom in his cell, again and again, always in that same cool tone, even when he screamed and begged for mercy.

"My name is Hailey Sumner," said the woman, waving a chrome-plated handgun. "You made quite a mess for us back there."

"Please," said Tetris. "He's hurt. We have to get him to a hospital. You can have me, I don't care, but we have to get him--"

"Who?" asked Hailey. "Oh, you mean him?"

She lifted the shiny pistol and shot Vincent in the head.

"Whoops," she said in the ringing silence that followed, as chunks of skull slid down Tetris's gasping cheeks. "Your friend didn't make it. That's too bad."

Before Tetris could form words or wipe the gore off his face or even force his lungs to draw breath, Dicer's macrognathic truck erupted from the darkness. Its huge tires spun as it arced through furious rifle fire. Sparks cascaded and vanished in the whirling snow. The scarred man stepped back from Tetris's window and raised his revolver.

Hollywood leaned out the truck's passenger-side window and fired a shotgun, unleashing a harsh light and a terrible crack that caught the scarred torturer in the chest and flung him to the ground. Dicer's truck smashed into the van blocking Tetris's way, knocking it aside. As Dicer reversed, the truck's exterior still popping and cracking with gunfire, the front bumper sloughed free.

Hailey Sumner had vanished.

"Go!" shouted Hollywood through the din.

Tetris went. He scraped the van on the way by but kept the pedal bottomed out, wrenching the car into the opposite lane. Three of the sedan's windows burst into shimmering ice. Tetris hunkered low behind the wheel as glass flechettes stung his brow and neck.

Just as he cleared the last van, he glimpsed Dicer's truck bouncing into the forest. Then his rearview mirror shattered. A giant hand seized the sedan and dragged it left with a banshee shriek. Popped tire, he thought in some region of his brain that was still functioning. He wrestled back onto the road and accelerated, but the wheel with the popped tire bounced and screeched on the asphalt. He flew around a bend and into the empty night, fighting the sedan as it tugged him left left left. Then he lost his resolve for just a moment and glanced at Vincent's limp form. The side of the agent's head was a horrible red bowl.

When his eyes returned to the spiderwebbed windshield, Tetris found the forest rushing up before him. He twirled the wheel back toward the center of the road, but not fast enough, as the sedan leapt the rumble strips, vaulted the shoulder, and went tumbling down the slope into stumps and saplings and bushes and rocks and gullies and cool, merciful silence.

*****

For the first time since his transformation, Tetris dreamed.

He climbed a tree in the depths of the forest, hand over hand, grasping tiny outcroppings of bark, tangling his fingers in nests of tough moss. The trunk was so wide that its curve was barely noticeable, like the curve of an empty horizon. There were smells, loam and living wood and the distant fecund sweetness of decay, but no sounds. He climbed and climbed, making no progress at all, until suddenly he reached the top.

As he penetrated the final leaf layer, he caught the herbal aroma of fresh thyme, carried across the canopy by a whispering breeze. The moon overhead was close and huge. He inclined his nose, sniffing, to find the source of the wonderful redolence, and came face to face with an enormous white moth.

He staggered and fell back into the canopy. Somehow he arrested his descent, cradled amid the soft leaves. He clambered back up. The moth was still there, its antennae bent pensively. It was furry; its compound eyes were matte black orbs.

"Hmmmmmmmmm," hummed the moth.

Tetris sat cross-legged a few feet away.

"I know you," said the moth.

"Of course you do," said Tetris. "What are you trying to tell me?"

The moth fanned its variegated wings, obscuring the sky, before resettling them with a barely audible sigh. "I don't . . . know."

Tetris looked at the stars. Or where the stars were supposed to be, anyway. There was really only one star, to the left of the leering moon, and it was dim and distant. He stared at the lonely star. When he began to feel that it was staring back, he tore his uneasy eyes away.

"If this is a vision, and you're trying to tell me

something, you should just tell me," said Tetris.

"Who do you think I am, again?" asked the moth.

"The forest," said Tetris.

The moth was quiet for a long time.

"I don't think so," it said.

"Then who?"

"I'm not sure," said the moth, looking past him at the rolling canopy, the treetops blue hills in the meager light. Everything else was dark, but the moth shone with captured moonlight. "Still. I know you."

Tetris's tree began to sink into the depths, but he couldn't find the will to uncross his legs and climb to another one.

"Wait," he shouted, as the moth dwindled above him. "Wait!"

Then darkness swallowed him, and the dreamscape descended into inchoate madness, screeches and black shapes and bristling slender teeth.

*****

The world was light. Hot, candent, electrified light. Tetris opened his eyes a sliver and closed them again. His body felt like a single enormous, lumpy bruise. Thoughts pinged against the walls of his skull, shuddered in the grogginess and thumping pain, and deliquesced.

"Where," he said, and tried opening his eyes again.

His pupils, normally elastic, were slow to contract. Gradually an image emerged: white walls, white-curtained window blazing with light, white rails on the bed atop which he lay. White sheets and a shining white-labeled IV bag swaying as he moved.

In the corner, above and to the left: a square television, the boxy old vacuum-tube kind, volume set to "insistent murmur," displaying a news program, plastic smiles above a glass and steel desk.

Tetris tried to move his legs and found them restrained by leather straps. His arms leapt against similar restraints. The IV pinched his arm.

"He lives," said the man beside the bed, folding his newspaper and handing it to a tall man beside him. A curled black cord led from the tall man's cauliflower ear down the back of his bridge-cable neck.

Tetris screwed his eyes shut again and reached out to the forest. He found nothing except the musk of distant, amorphous fear.

"My name is Don McCarthy," said the man, waving a hand over Tetris's closed eyes. Inside Tetris's lids, the hand was a dark shadow flitting across a webbed green plain. "Hello? Anybody in there? I'm the Secretary of State."

"Toni Davis," said Tetris.

"Is deceased, I'm afraid," said McCarthy, sitting in a metal chair turned backwards, his legs sprawled wide. His eyes were small and sharp as polished onyx. His hair was close-cropped and gray. "I've got her job now."

"Who are you?"

McCarthy waved at the bodyguard. "Leave us alone,

please."

The man left after a glance through his impenetrable sunglasses.

"I used to be in charge of the Coast Guard," said McCarthy. "Lousy job. Nobody appreciates what you do. One monster slips by and gobbles a grandmother out walking her poodle, and they're after your head. Doesn't matter that you stopped another fifty earlier that week. Zero tolerance for error. Sensationalist media." He sighed. "It goes without saying, but I like being Secretary of State a whole lot better."

"Vincent," said Tetris.

"He's dead," said McCarthy, raising a finger. "Also Dale Cooper. Jack Dano." He ticked them off. "Davis. Bunch of government aides. Scientists. Plus a couple thousand innocents in Portugal, and our man in Atlantic City." His hands fluttered amusedly. "It's a funny thing, Mr. Aphelion, the way everyone around you seems to expire."

Tetris drove his head against the white metal bars at the head of the cot. An animal grunt escaped his clamped teeth.

"Well," said McCarthy, leaning in conspiratorially, "I suppose I can't pin all of those on you. A few of them are my fault."

Tetris stopped moving.

"I took your plane down, pal."

The Secretary's breath was foul. Tetris tried not to inhale.

"With national security at stake," said McCarthy, "we

really had no other option."

"You killed them," said Tetris. His side hurt.

McCarthy stood. "I knew what you were the moment I heard about you," he said. "The moment you walked out of the forest, I knew. Knew you were the greatest threat mankind had ever seen."

Tetris spasmed against the bonds.

"I pity you, Aphelion. I really do."

Tetris strained and strained, but the shackles remained firm.

"You let this thing into your mind," said McCarthy, circling the bed. "You believed its lies. Aliens. Invasions. You should have died like a man in the forest. Instead you gave in, came here, and spread your disease. You worked for the enemy. You deceived the Secretary of State. Do you have any idea the work it's taken to undo the damage from those lies?"

"What lies?"

"There are no aliens," said McCarthy. "There's no invasion."

Tetris fell back, heart banging away. "No."

"We looked. There isn't anything out there."

"It's too far," said Tetris. "It's six years away."

McCarthy spat a bitter laugh. "Six years! Time. That's all it wanted. Time to figure out how to kill us without us killing it first. You never questioned it, did you? Not even once."

"Are you listening to this?" Tetris asked the ceiling. "Hello?"

"It's listening," said McCarthy, "even if it pretends it's not."

"You're wrong," said Tetris. "If there wasn't an invasion coming, the forest would already have killed us."

"How?"

"Toxins. Pods of toxins, all over the world. It showed me, in a vision."

"Toxins delivered on what? The air?" McCarthy laughed. "You know how long it would take a cloud of gas to drift on wind currents across an entire continent? Do you—I mean, have you heard of gas masks? Hazmat suits? We would fire our missiles before it did more than tickle New York."

Tetris arced against his bonds, ignoring the blinding pain in his side.

"You idiot," said McCarthy, "it knows we can kill it, and it's playing for more time. All of this, it's a trick. You fell for it. And so did Davis, and Dano, and everyone else on that plane. You all fell for it. But not me."

"You're wrong," said Tetris, although suddenly he wasn't sure.

"Can you believe you got all your friends killed?" He shook his head sadly. "I can't believe it, personally. Some of them were my friends too."

Tetris saw spiders and snakes tearing into masses of soldiers, saw his own hands fling a man into the mouth of a tarantula. McCarthy's phone buzzed, and buzzed, and buzzed again.

"Why won't you answer me?" Tetris shouted at the

ceiling. "Where are you?"

Then the forest was there, filling its corner of his vibrating skull.

Look at the television, it said.

Tetris looked. "Please tell me that's one of yours."

That, said the forest, *has nothing to do with me*.

McCarthy looked too. The phone fell from his hand.

Ten minutes later, when Li and Dr. Alvarez came swinging through the window in a storm of rainbow shards, they found the room deserted, the bed wheeled away, chairs askew, an IV bag leaking a broadening puddle.

Li stowed her gun and ransacked the room for clues. She peered into the hall, checked the corners, and was getting down to explore the space beneath the dresser when Dr. Alvarez laid a hand on her shoulder.

Together they stood, in a room reeking of ammonia, as on the boxy black television something obscenely huge, hundreds of feet tall, raised its head out of billowing meteorite smoke. The head was followed by immeasurable chthonic bulk, size the camera could not capture, swing wildly though it did; and after the head and the bulk, when the too-numerous arms emerged, it became clear, to Li and Dr. Alvarez and all the others watching the grainy vision creeping across their screens, that this section of cratered Kansas farmland had become something terrible, a place of sulfurous fumes and apocalypse, a wasteland that could bear no possible name but Hell.

About the Author

Justin Groot lives in Southern California, where he spends most of his free time reading, writing, playing videogames, and rock climbing.

Twitter: @JustinGroot3

57426748R00182